Bar Brawl . . .

He looked back toward the barkeep, who had ducked down behind the bar.

"Oh, there you are," he said easily. "Could I have another beer, please?"

"Mister, are you crazy?" the barkeep hissed up at him. He was waving for Joe to get away. "You had better get out of the line of fire!"

"What line of fire?" Joe asked innocently.

"Didn't you just hear what Tyrell said? He's going to shoot your brother!"

Joe chuckled, then looked around toward Tyrell, who was standing about twenty feet away, his arm crooked and his hand opening and closing nervously just above the handle of his pistol.

"You ain't talking about that little pissant standing over there, are you?" Joe asked calmly.

"Oh, my, you shouldn't have said that," the bartender said in a frightened voice.

"Hell, mister, there ain't no call for you to be worryin' about him. We ain't in no line of fire. As soon as he twitches, Win will kill him. Now, how about that beer?"

DON'T MISS THESE
ALL-ACTION WESTERN SERIES
FROM THE BERKLEY PUBLISHING GROUP

THE GUNSMITH by J. R. Roberts
Clint Adams was a legend among lawmen, outlaws, and ladies. They called him . . . the Gunsmith.

LONGARM by Tabor Evans
The popular long-running series about U.S. Deputy Marshal Long—his life, his loves, his fight for justice.

SLOCUM by Jake Logan
Today's longest-running action Western. John Slocum rides a deadly trail of hot blood and cold steel.

BUSHWHACKERS by B. J. Lanagan
An all-new series by the creators of Longarm! The rousing adventures of the most brutal gang of cutthroats ever assembled—Quantrill's Raiders.

BUSHWHACKERS

REBEL COUNTY

B. J. Lanagan

JOVE BOOKS, NEW YORK

REBEL COUNTY

A Jove Book / published by arrangement with
the author

PRINTING HISTORY
Jove edition / September 1997

The Putnam Berkley World Wide Web site address is
http://www.berkley.com

ISBN: 0-515-12142-8

A JOVE BOOK®
Jove Books are published by The Berkley Publishing Group,
200 Madison Avenue, New York, New York 10016,
a member of Penguin Putnam Inc.
JOVE and the "J" design are trademarks
belonging to Jove Publications, Inc.

PRINTED IN THE UNITED STATES OF AMERICA

10 9 8 7 6 5 4 3 2 1

BUSHWHACKERS

REBEL COUNTY

County Courthouse, San Saba, Texas

"HEAR YE! HEAR YE! HEAR YE! THIS, HERE TRIAL IS about to commence, the Honorable Douglas Canaby presidin'," the bailiff shouted. "Everybody stand respectful."

The Honorable Douglas Canaby came out of a back room. After taking his seat at the bench, he adjusted the glasses on the end of his nose, then cleared his throat.

"Would the bailiff please bring the accused before the bench?"

The bailiff, who was leaning against the side wall, spit a quid of tobacco into the brass spittoon, then walked over to the table where the defendant, Ray Kingsley, sat next to his court-appointed lawyer, Arnold Fenton.

"Get up, you," he growled. "Present yourself before the judge."

Ray was handcuffed, and had shackles on his ankles. He shuffled up to stand in front of the judge. Fenton went with him.

"Ray Kingsley, you stand accused of the crime of ridin' for that butcherin', thievin', rapin' bastard Quantrill," the judge said. "How do you plead?"

"Quantrill never raped nobody," Ray said. "It was only the red-legged Yankee bastards done that."

"How do you plead?" the judge asked again.

"Your Honor, if it please the court," Fenton said.

"You got somethin' to say to this court, Mr. Fenton?" Judge Canaby asked.

"Yes, Your Honor. Quantrill did most of his murderin' and thievin' up in Kansas and Missouri," the lawyer said.

"What's your point, Mr. Fenton?"

"Well, Your Honor, this here is Texas. Don't know why we're tryin' Mr. Kingsley in Texas for any murderin' and thievin' he might have done while he was up in Kansas. I move that this case be dismissed for lack of proper jurisdiction."

"Your Honor, it is known that Quantrill spent one winter in Texas," the prosecutor said.

"There you go," Judge Canaby said, slapping his gavel on the bench. "If Quantrill was down here, that gives me all the jurisdiction I need."

"But Your Honor, these were his own people. He didn't do no murderin' nor thievin' while he was down here."

"None that we know of, Your Honor," the prosecutor replied quickly. "And I hasten to remind Your Honor we're tryin' this defendant for being one of Quantrill's riders, not for any specific act of murder or robbery he may have done. Therefore, the fact that Quantrill was once in Texas, and that this defendant was with him, puts the case under your jurisdiction."

The judge slapped his gavel on the bench again. "You are right, Mr. Prosecutor. Mr. Fenton, your motion for dismissal is denied. This case shall proceed."

"Very well, Your Honor."

"How do you plead?"

"Your Honor, my client pleads guilty and he throws himself upon the mercy of the court."

"Wait a minute, hold on there!" Ray shouted. "I ain't pleadin' guilty to nothin'!"

The judge glared. "Did you or did you not confess before several assembled men in the Red Dog Saloon last night that you rode with Quantrill?"

"That wasn't a confession, Judge," Ray said. "I was just drinkin' and talkin' and tellin' war stories with some of the other fellas, that's all."

"And during the course of your talking, did you say you rode with Quantrill?" the judge asked.

Ray looked at his lawyer. "I don't know much about the law, but ain't there somethin' says I don't have to answer questions like that?"

"That's right," the lawyer agreed. "It's called the Fifth Amendment, and it says you don't have to answer any question that may incriminate you."

Ray smiled. "That's what I'm goin' to do then. I ain't goin' to answer that question."

"Very well," the judge said. "Clerk, change Mr. Kingsley's plea from guilty to not guilty."

"You're making a big mistake, Mr. Kingsley," Fenton whispered to him. "I know this judge. If you plead guilty, he might show you some mercy. If you're found guilty, you'll get none."

"Well, what can happen to me? I mean, even if I did ride with Quantrill, what can he do to me besides tell me I can't vote or hold office or something like that? Hell, I never signed no loyalty oath to the goddamn Yankee government, so I can't do none of that anyway."

"Oh, Mr. Kingsley, he can do a lot more than that to you," Fenton said ominously.

"What else can he do?"

"He can hang you."

Ray gasped, then put his hand to his throat. "Hang me?" he asked in a choked voice.

"That's right."

Ray looked back up toward the bench. "Judge, I want to change my plea again!" he said.

"Too late for that, boy, we've done entered your plea of not guilty," Judge Canaby said. "Mr. Prosecutor, are you prepared to make your case?"

"I am, Your Honor. You men over there," the prosecutor said, pointing to several men sitting in the front row. "You are all my witnesses. Stand up and hold up your right hand."

The men did as they were instructed, and the clerk swore them in.

"Now," the prosecutor said. "Did all of you hear this man say last night that he had ridden for Quantrill?"

All the witnesses nodded yes, or answered in the affirmative.

The prosecutor turned back toward the judge. "Well, there you are, Your Honor. Every one of these men have just sworn that they heard the defendant admit to being one of Quantrill's riders during the war."

"Mr. Fenton, do you have anything to say in defense of this wretched soul who is your client?"

"Your Honor, I know that you and the sheriff and every-one else of authority in this county are Yankees, appointed to office by the Federal Government as part of our recon-struction," Fenton said. "But if you would just look out into the gallery you'll see men and women who were born and raised here. They are good people, Southerners by birth, and during the late unpleasantness they were South-erners by loyalty. If you ask them to pass judgment against a man, simply because he fought for what he believed in,

I believe you are going to find that they will think Mr. Kingsley was just a soldier doing his duty. And as you have come to live among us, I ask that you pass judgment on this matter with some feeling for the sensitivities of those whom you now represent.''

The gallery broke into applause at Fenton's statement, and the judge angrily banged his gavel until they were quiet. ''I represent the Federal Government of the United States and her laws first,'' Judge Canaby replied, ''and the people and the laws of Texas second.'' Canaby looked over toward the jury.

''You gentlemen of the jury,'' he said. ''Do you go along with what these folks in the gallery believe? Do you think this man who rode with Quantrill was nothing more than a soldier doing his duty?''

''Your Honor, that's what we think, yes,'' one of the men in the jury said after taking a quick, visual poll of his fellow jurors.

''In other words, if you had to make a decision now, you would say not guilty?'' the judge asked.

The spokesman for the jury nodded. ''Yes, sir, Your Honor, that's what we would say, all right.''

Again everyone cheered, and Ray smiled broadly.

''Then you are all dismissed,'' the judge said angrily.

''Thank you, Your Honor,'' Fenton said, putting his hand on Ray's shoulder.

''No, not the defendant!'' the judge said. He pointed to the men in the jury box. ''I mean those Rebel bastards on the jury are dismissed. I will decide the case.''

''You, Your Honor?''

''Do you see any other judge in this room, Mr. Fenton?''

''No, sir.''

''Then I will make the decision. In fact, I have already made the decision. Ray Kingsley, I find you guilty as charged. Now, you stand there while I administer the sentence."

"Your Honor, we beg for mercy," Fenton said.

Judge Canaby fixed Fenton with an intense scowl as he took off his glasses and began polishing them. Then he looked back at Kingsley and cleared his throat.

"Ray Kingsley, you have been tried before me, and you have been found guilty of the crime of riding with the butcher Quantrill, and aiding and abetting in the atrocities of murder, arson, and robbery that he visited upon innocent people," Judge Canaby said. "Before this court passes sentence, have you anything to say?"

"Judge, all I can say is, I was just a soldier doin' my duty," Ray said. "I know they was lots of Yankee soldiers done just as bad, and some of 'em done worse, but they ain't no paper out on them like there is for thems of us that rode with Quantrill."

"You were just a soldier doing your duty, you say? Well, Mr. Kingsley, one day that duty included burning and sacking the town of Lawrence, Kansas. Do you recall that day, sir?"

"Yes, sir, I recall that."

"Were you present on that day?"

Ray cleared his throat. "Your Honor, I ain't goin' to lie to you," he said. "It ain't one of my proudest moments, but I was there that day."

"Lawrence, Kansas was a lovely, peaceful city, Mr. Kingsley, wherein resided my younger brother, his wife, and two sons. My brother and his two sons were murdered that day. And you, you miserable son of a bitch, whether you personally did it or not, were there when it happened."

Ray looked at the floor then, knowing that there was nothing more he could say, and knowing too that he could expect no mercy from this judge.

"Ray Kingsley, it is the sentence of this court that you be taken from this courthouse and put in jail. I further direct the constable of this town to build, or cause to be built, a gallows or some other device, fixture, apparatus, contrivance, agent, or whatever means as may be sufficient to suspend your carcass above the ground. When the machine is completed you are to be taken from jail to that contrivance, where you will have a noose placed around your neck. You will then be dropped through a trapdoor, which will bring about the effect of breaking your neck, collapsing your windpipe, and in any and all ways squeezing the last breath of life from your worthless, vile, and miserable body.''

"No!'' someone in the court shouted. "You can't hang him, you Yankee bastard! He ain't guilty of nothin' but bein' a soldier!''

"Constable!'' the judge said. "Arrest the man who just made that outburst and hold him in contempt of court!''

The constable stood and looked out over the gallery. "Arrest which man, Judge?'' the constable asked. "I didn't see who it was.''

To a man, every person in the courtroom at that moment was quiet.

"Who was it?'' the judge asked. "Who made that outburst?''

There was no response to his inquiry.

"All right, all right!'' the judge said. "You Rebel bastards think you are putting one over on me. But we'll see who has the last laugh when this miserable bastard is hanged. Constable, I leave the prisoner in your hands. You are to watch over him until the sentence is carried out.''

"Yes, sir,'' the constable said.

"In the meantime I had best hurry down to the depot and catch the train when it returns to Lampassas.''

The judge, the sheriff, and the bailiff hurried out the back door then, leaving the courtroom under the control of the city constable. Unlike the three officers of the court, Constable Gibson was a native Texan and personally sympathetic to the lost cause of the South.

"Goddamn, Gibson, you ain't goin' to hang this boy, are you?" someone called.

"You heard the judge, Andrew," Gibson replied. "He give me the order. There ain't nothin' I can do about it."

"Son of a bitch! Hangin' a man just 'cause he soldiered for the wrong side. That ain't right!"

"Come on, Fenton," the constable said. "You've got to help me get this prisoner back into jail."

The crowd booed, and shouted angry curses at the constable and the lawyer as Gibson and Fenton began escorting Ray back to the jail cell. But though the mood of the crowd was ugly, they made no attempt to try to rescue Ray Kingsley.

2

WIN COULTER WAS WALKING BEHIND A MULE, WATCHING the dirt fold away from the plowshare as it opened a deep, new farrow. A few yards in front of him his younger brother, Joe, was plowing another furrow, while a few yards behind, their father was breaking open a third row. Half the field had already been tilled, and the coal-black dirt glistened with the nutrients that made the soil so fertile.

Win looked over toward the two-story white house where they all lived, and at the barn, granary, and machine shed that made up the Coulter farm. The windows in the house were shining brightly in the sunlight first silver, then gold, then red. The color spread from the windows to the side of the house, then to the roof, and then to the other buildings. But as the color intensified, Win was shocked to see that it wasn't reflected sunlight at all.

It was fire!

The house, barn, and all the outbuildings were engulfed in a blazing inferno!

Win looked back toward his father and gasped, for his father was now a human torch. Flames were leaping up from his body, yet he continued to walk behind the plow, as if totally unconcerned that he was being consumed by fire.

"Joe! Joe!" Win shouted.

"I'M RIGHT HERE, WIN," JOE'S CALM VOICE ANSWERED.

Win looked up with a start and saw his brother's concerned face. Now, outside sounds intruded . . . the rattle and squeak of a train in motion, the rhythmic clicking of wheels over track joints, the conversations of other passengers. Time and place returned, and he realized that this wasn't pre-war Missouri, this was post-war Texas.

"Are you all right?" Joe asked.

Win ran his hand across his face, as if wiping the sleep away. "Yeah," he answered. He sat up. "Yeah, I'm all right."

"Did you have that dream again?"

Win nodded without speaking.

"Win, there wasn't nothin' we coulda done," Joe reminded him. "The Jayhawkers come to the farm while we was gone. They killed Ma and Pa and burned the place. You got to get over feelin' guilty about it."

"If I hadn't stayed for one more day of drinkin' and cardplayin', we would've been there."

"It wasn't just you wanted to stay," Joe reminded him. "I was with you, remember? And I was enjoyin' the trip just as much as you. But that was a long time ago."

"Yeah, I know it was a long time ago."

"I don't know why this has been botherin' you so much lately. You didn't have these dreams durin' the war."

"During the war we were with Quantrill and we were doing something about it."

"I reckon we done our own share of burnin' and killin' then," Joe said.

Win looked out the window and saw nothing but mesquite and dirt sliding by under the late afternoon sun. He didn't believe he had ever seen anything as God-awful-ugly as West Texas.

The view inside wasn't all that attractive either. It consisted mostly of overweight drummers and washed-out, poor immigrant families. It had improved somewhat when a young woman had gotten on the train a couple of hours earlier. When she'd boarded she'd smiled at Win while passing by, looking for a seat.

Somewhat later a young, sandy-haired cowboy, wearing an ivory-handled pistol, leather chaps, and highly polished silver rowels, had gotten on the train. He'd swaggered back and forth through the car a few times before finally settling in a seat next to the pretty young woman. They were sitting together when Win dozed off.

Now, as Win looked toward them, he saw that though they were still together, the young woman did not appear to be enjoying the cowboy's company. She got up and changed seats, but it was to no avail, as the cowboy also changed seats to be near her. The young woman got up again, and this time she stepped out onto the vestibule. The cowboy waited for a moment, then got up as well and followed her outside.

Win turned his attention away from them. "Where are we anyway?" he asked.

"We're nearly there. I just heard the conductor say we'd be coming into San Saba in a few minutes," Joe answered.

"And Ray is going to meet us?"

"That's what his letter said. He said he has a deal that is too sweet for us to pass up."

"I hope it's not bullshit."

"Ray was always pretty dependable, remember? When he came back with a scouting report, we could always count on what he said," Joe said.

"That's true," Win agreed. He stretched, then stood up. "I think I'll go out onto the vestibule and get a breath of air."

"Don't fall off," Joe quipped.

Win smiled, then picked his way forward through the rattling, rocking car. When he stepped outside he saw that the pretty young woman was still being harassed by the cowboy.

"Please," the girl was saying. "Please, just leave me alone."

"Who do you think you're foolin' by bein' so high-and-mighty?" the cowboy asked. "I know who you are, and I know what you are."

"I am someone who wants to be left alone," the woman said.

Win looked over toward them to measure the sincerity in the woman's voice. He was hesitant to butt into anyone else's business, but the woman was clearly having a hard time with the cowboy.

"Mister, why don't you go away and leave the lady alone?" Win said.

The cowboy looked toward Win as if shocked that anyone would have the audacity to interfere.

"What did you just say to me?"

"I told you to leave the lady alone."

"Why don't you just go to Hell?" the cowboy growled menacingly. He turned back to the girl, as if dismissing Win out of hand. Win stepped across the gap between them and grabbed the cowboy by the scruff of the neck and the seat of his pants.

"Hey, what the . . ." the cowboy shouted, but whatever the fourth word was going to be was lost in the rattle of cars and the cowboy's own surprised scream as Win threw the young man bodily from the train. The cowboy hit on the down-slope of the track base, then bounced and rolled through the rocks and scrub-weed alongside the track. Win leaned out far enough to see him stand up and shake his fist, but by then the train had swept on away from him.

"He'll be all right," Win said. "He'll have a little walk into town, is all."

The girl laughed, and even above the sound of the train Win could hear the musical lilt to her laugh. Joe stepped out onto the platform at that moment.

"What is it?" Joe asked. "What happened?"

"The fella with all the silver just got off the train," Win said easily. He looked at the girl. "Do you know him?"

"Yes. His name is Tyrell. Tim Tyrell. He works for Jason Bellefontaine."

"I never stopped to think that you might know him. I hope I wasn't out of line. I hope you were serious when you told him to leave you alone."

"I was very serious, and you weren't out of line at all," she said.

The train started slowing.

"This is it," Joe said. "Our stop."

"Oh!" the girl said. "You are getting off here?"

"Yes," Win answered.

"So am I. Maybe we'll see each other again," she suggested hopefully.

Win smiled, and touched the brim of his hat. "You can count on it," he said.

"Come on, Big Brother," Joe said. "We have to see to our horses."

Joe's reference to Win as "Big Brother" stemmed from the fact that Win was older, not from their relative size.

Win was a leather-tough and wiry five feet eight, with ash-blond hair and blue eyes. He was the kind of man women considered good-looking, but there was also a quality about him that frightened them, as if they could see a flash of hellfire in his eyes.

Joe was the younger of the two, but at a very muscular six foot one and nearly two hundred pounds, he was also bigger. His hair was much darker than his brother's, but his eyes were exactly the same color and had the same flash of hellfire.

SOME FIFTEEN MINUTES LATER, WIN AND JOE HAD THEIR horses off the stock car and saddled as the train, its whistle blowing, bell ringing, and steam puffing, started chugging around the wide circle of track that would start it back in the other direction, San Saba being the end of the line. The brothers walked the horses off the wooden loading platform, and were about to mount when Joe caught sight of a wall filled with wanted posters.

"Win, wait," he said, pointing. "Think we ought to take a look at them wanted posters?"

"Probably wouldn't be a bad idea," Win agreed. They walked over for a closer perusal.

"Look at this," Joe said.

WANTED
FOR MURDER, TRAIN AND BANK ROBBERY
$500 DOLLAR REWARD
DEAD OR ALIVE
THE OUTLAWS
WIN AND JOE COULTER
FORMER GUERRILLAS WITH
QUANTRILL'S RAIDERS

"Murder? We've done our share of killing," Win said. "Don't know as I'd call it murder."

"Didn't know there was paper on us this far out," Joe said.

Win looked around, and seeing that he wasn't being observed, tore off the circular. "Long as there are no pictures or descriptions, we've got nothing to worry about," he said.

"I reckon not," Joe agreed.

As the noise of the receding train faded, it was replaced by the sound of hammering and sawing.

"Sounds like some building goin' on," Win said. "Must be a busy little town."

"Ray said it was," Joe said. "By the way, where is he? I thought he was going to meet us."

"Yeah, so did I. But I sure as hell don't see him."

"So, what do we do now?"

"Maybe he had to go somewhere. Best thing for us to do is board our horses, get us a room in the hotel, then wait around a few days."

As Win was talking, the young woman he had rescued on the train walked by. She nodded in his direction, then smiled again.

Joe chuckled. "From the looks of things, waitin' around may not be all that hard for you," he suggested.

"We do what we can, Little Brother, to while away the hours," Win teased.

The two brothers mounted and started toward the stable. When they reached the street side of the depot, they saw the cause of the construction sounds they had been hearing. At the far end of the street, a gallows was being built.

"I'll be damned," Joe said. "Look at that. I wonder who it's for?"

"Why don't we ride down there and ask?"

There were two carpenters up on the platform itself, and a third down on the ground, sawing boards at a sawhorse.

Half a dozen young boys, barefooted and with ragged bottoms to their pants, stood around watching.

"You boys get away from here," a large, middle-aged man shouted to the youngsters. "This ain't no place for you. What are you doin' out here anyway? Your mamas will be setting supper to the table soon."

"We want to see the hangin'," one of the boys answered.

"Well, there ain't goin' to be no hangin' today, so why don't you go on. Get away and let these men get their work done!"

The man who was shouting was wearing a badge. He looked up at Win and Joe, and as they were mounted, the action caused him to have to look into the brightness of the sky behind them. He squinted.

"Don't know you two fellas, do I?" he asked.

"We just come in," Joe answered.

"So it's already started, has it?"

"I beg your pardon?" Win asked. "What has already started?"

"Folks comin' in to see the hangin'. Well, I'll tell you just like I told these kids. The hangin' ain't until tomorrow."

"You the sheriff?" Win asked.

"I'm the town constable. The name's Gibson. Charley Gibson. Used to be sheriff of San Saba County, but I wouldn't swear no oath of loyalty to the goddamn Yankee government, so I can't be sheriff no more." He spat a quid of tobacco, then wiped the residue from his chin with the back of his hand.

Win nodded toward the gallows. "Truth is, we didn't know anything about the hangin'. It's tomorrow, you say?"

"The lynchin' takes place tomorrow afternoon at two o'clock."

Curious at Gibson's remark, Win twisted in his saddle for another look at the gallows.

"Lynching? Never heard of building a gallows for a lynching," he said. "Always thought they used something like a stout tree limb, or a telegraph pole, for things like that."

"Yeah, well, you might call this hangin' a *legal* lynchin'. It's legal 'cause they was a trial, if you can call what they had for this fella a trial."

"You sayin' he didn't get a fair trial?"

"Ain't my place to say," Gibson answered.

"Sure it is. You are an officer of the law, aren't you?"

"I told you, I'm just the town constable. The real law around here belongs to Jason Bellefontaine."

"Jason Bellefontaine?"

"You know him?"

"I'm not sure," Win answered. He remembered the girl telling him that the cowboy he threw off the train worked for Jason Bellefontaine. "I believe I've heard that name somewhere before. It's the second time I've heard it today. Who is he?"

"He was some Yankee bigwig during the war," Gibson answered. "They say he was a general, but I don't know if he was a fightin' general."

Win snapped his fingers. "The Kansas Tenth," he said. "I *have* heard of him. He was their general, but he never rode with them."

"That's him, all right."

"What's he doing down here in Texas?"

"He come down here after the war with a carpetbag full of government warrants and bills, and he's turned all those Yankee laws into Yankee dollars."

"Sounds like a fella could get rich doing that," Joe suggested.

"He's rich enough to buy up half the land in the county."

"And the law?" Win asked.

Gibson nodded. "And the law."

"It's just a guess, Constable, but I'd say he hasn't bought you," Win said.

Gibson snorted. "Hell, what would the son of a bitch want with me? I ain't worth his money. I don't do nothin' more'n run away pesky kids, or now and again throw a drunk in jail to sleep it off."

"This fella they're hangin' tomorrow. They keeping him in your jail?" Win asked.

Gibson nodded. "Yeah, a man by the name of Ray Kingsley. You ever heard of him?"

Win and Joe exchanged a quick, secretive look. Ray Kingsley was the man they were there to meet.

"No, never heard of him," Win replied. "What did he do?"

"Do? Hell, he didn't do nothin' but get drunk the other night and tell some folks he once rode with Quantrill. Seems like our sheriff and judge have a special hatred for anyone who ever rode with Quantrill. They've got ever' poster ever put out on any of 'em, includin' some, I think, that was put out durin' the war. Truth is, most of those wanted posters wouldn't be given a second look in any other county but San Saba. Makes no difference to our judge and sheriff, though. If a man rode for Quantrill, he'd be a lot better off if he'd just stay away from here."

"I don't understand that. This bein' a Southern town, why would your judge and sheriff have such a special hatred for Quantrill's men?" Joe asked.

" 'Cause neither one of them are Southerners. They was both appointed to their offices down here. The judge was a lawyer somewhere up in Kansas. And the sheriff was a first sergeant in the Tenth Kansas.''

''Bellefontaine's division?'' Win asked.

''Now you're beginning to catch on,'' Gibson said. ''The judge and the sheriff come down here with Bellfontaine and the other carpetbaggers. Just like buzzards, they've started pickin' the carcass clean. By now, they've pretty near taken over all of West Texas . . . stealin' land for back taxes and buying up businesses for pennies on the dollar.''

''What do the locals think of it?''

''The real folk—that is, the decent folk in this town— still have a lot of hard feelings against the Yankees, especially them that have come down here to take over things. And if you'd ask one of them, they'd likely tell you that Quantrill, Bloody Bill Anderson, and others like them was patriots, and Ray Kingsley and them that rode with Quantrill was brave men.''

''Glad to hear that,'' Win said.

''You boys wasn't with Quantrill, was you?'' Gibson held up his hand almost as soon as he asked the question. ''No,'' he said. ''Don't answer that. It would be better all around. But unless I miss my guess, you two was in the war yourselves.''

''Yes,'' Win said.

''You don't sound Texan, though. More like Arkansas, or Missouri,'' Gibson said.

''Could be either one,'' Joe said.

''I'd be careful 'bout who I told that to. Quantrill was in Missouri.''

''So was Sterling Price, General Van Dorn, Jo Shelby, Jeff Thompson, and several others,'' Win replied.

''What do you say we just let it go at that?'' Gibson suggested.

''I'd say that was a good idea,'' Win said.

"You boys plannin' on staying around for a while?"

"A couple of days maybe. I see the Red Dog across the street. Is that a pretty good place to wet a whistle?"

"If you don't mind givin' your money to General Belle-fontaine," Gibson said. "If you're more partial to a South-ern patriot, you might try Matt's Place, just up the street a ways. His whiskey ain't watered and he's a good man."

"Thanks," Win said, touching the brim of his hat and turning his mount away.

"WHAT ARE WE GOIN' TO DO ABOUT RAY, WIN?" JOE asked quietly as they rode away.

"Don't know as there's anything we can do about it," Win replied.

"I hate to just stand by and watch him hang."

"We're on the wrong side of the law, Little Brother. When you're on this side, hangin' is a risk we all take."

Instinctively, Joe reached up to pull his shirt collar away from his neck.

3

WIN AND JOE PUT THEIR HORSES UP AT THE LIVERY, THEN walked across the street to the saloon known as Matt's Place. It was not yet supper time, and a little early for peak business, so the saloon was only about one-third full. The scarred piano sat unused in the back of the room. There were two saloon girls working the customers, but they were occupied by a table full of men.

"Two beers," Win ordered, sliding a piece of silver across the bar. The man behind the bar drew two mugs and set them, with foaming heads, in front of the brothers. They drank the first ones down without taking away the mugs. Then they wiped the foam away from their lips and slid the empty mugs back toward the barkeep.

"That one was for thirst," Win explained. "This will be for taste. Do it again."

Smiling, the bartender gave them a second round.

With the beer in his hand, Win turned his back to the bar and looked out over the saloon. Noticing them then, one of the two girls pulled herself away from the table and sidled up to the two brothers. She had bleached hair and was heavily painted, but behind her tired eyes was a suggestion of good humor. She smiled at Joe.

"What a handsome devil you are," she said. "I'll just bet you've broken many a poor girl's heart."

"I've bent them around a few times," Joe quipped. "Don't know as I ever broke any."

The girl laughed. "My name's Sandra," she said. "What's yours?"

"Joe." Joe turned toward the bartender. "It looks to me like this lovely young lady needs a drink."

"Coming right up," the bartender said, filling a glass from Sandra's special bottle.

It was at that moment that the bat-wing doors swung open, and the cowboy in black and silver came in. He had scratches and bruises on his face, and his clothes were dirty and torn.

"You lost, Tyrell? This ain't the Red Dog," someone said.

Tyrell glared at the speaker, and that was when everyone noticed his condition.

"Jesus! What the hell happened to you?" someone asked.

"Some son of a bitch pushed me off the train," Tyrell growled.

Everyone laughed.

Tyrell started to say something else, then saw Win standing quietly at the bar, calmly drinking his beer. He pointed his finger at him.

"You!" he shouted. He was so choked with anger that he could barely get the words out. "You're the one who did this to me!"

"Did you have a nice walk into town, Tyrell?" Win asked easily. He took another swallow of his beer, then pulled the mug back down and wiped the back of his hand across his mouth. "Why don't you have a beer on me? You could probably use one."

"You son of a bitch! You offer me a beer? You offer me a beer and think I'll forget about what you did to me? What the hell got into you, mister, to do a damn thing like that?"

"Back where I come from, when a lady asks a man to leave, he does," Win said. "Since you didn't leave when she asked you, I figured maybe you could use a little lesson in manners."

Again everyone laughed.

"Is that what this is all about, Tyrell? Teaching you some manners?" someone asked.

"We'll see who is the teacher and who is the pupil around here," Tyrell said. "I'm going to teach this bastard never to butt into anyone else's business again." He grinned evilly. "Only the lesson ain't goin' to do him no good, 'cause he's going to be dead. Pull your gun, mister! Pull your gun! I'm goin' to shoot your eyes out now!"

The laughter stopped then. This had gone beyond joking and, anticipating a killing, there was a quick scrape of chairs and tables as everyone, including Sandra, scrambled to get out of the way.

Joe was the only one who didn't move away from Win.

"Looks like he don't want your beer," Joe said nonchalantly.

"I reckon not."

"I'll take it then," Joe said calmly. He looked back toward the barkeep, who had ducked down behind the bar.

"Oh, there you are," he said easily. "Could I have another beer, please?"

"Mister, are you crazy?" the barkeep hissed up at him. He was waving for Joe to get away. "You had better get out of the line of fire!"

"What line of fire?" Joe asked innocently.

"Didn't you just hear what Tyrell said? He's going to shoot your brother!"

Joe chuckled, then looked around toward Tyrell, who was standing about twenty feet away, his arm crooked and his hand opening and closing nervously just above the handle of his pistol.

"You ain't talking about that little pissant standing over there, are you?" Joe asked calmly.

"Oh, my, you shouldn't have said that," the bartender said in a frightened voice.

"Hell, mister, there ain't no call for you to be worryin' about him. We ain't in no line of fire. As soon as he twitches, Win will kill him. Now, how about that beer?"

"Beer?" the bartender repeated, as if unable to believe Joe's total lack of concern for what was happening.

"Yes, and listen," Joe went on, as if the next beer was much more important than the impending gun battle. "When you draw my beer this time, could you tip the mug a little so's there isn't quite as much foam? I swear, that last one was mostly head."

Several people gasped. They were as surprised as the bartender by Joe's easy words and calm manner.

The barkeep didn't move.

"What about it? Do you get me another beer, or do I have to draw it myself?"

Raising himself just far enough to take the mug, the bartender quickly drew another beer, then set it on the bar and ducked down again.

"Thanks," Joe said. He blew the foam off, then turned around. He was still standing right next to Win, clearly in the line of fire if a gunfight should break out. He took a swallow of his beer and stared across the room at Tyrell.

Tyrell, like the others, had heard Joe's calm declaration.

It was beginning to have an effect on him, and his hands started shaking.

"Look at the little sonofabitch shake," Joe said. "Hell, you might as well go ahead and kill him and get it over with, Big Brother. Otherwise he's goin' to stand right there and piss in his pants."

"You're right," Win said. "All right, Tyrell, let's do it."

"No!" Tyrell suddenly screamed, holding his hands up. "No, I'm not going to draw on you!" He turned to face the others. "You are all my witnesses! I'm not going to fight!"

"If you aren't going to fight, then get the hell out of here," Win growled.

Tyrell licked his lips a couple of times, then turned and ran outside, chased out into the street by the laughter of everyone in the saloon.

"Step up to the bar, boys!" someone shouted. "The drinks are on the house! Anytime I can see one of Bellefontaine's boys backed down like that, it's worth a round."

"Beer!"

"Whiskey!"

More than a dozen voices called out their orders as everyone rushed to the bar. The man who had offered to buy the drinks came down from the stairs where he had been a witness to what just transpired. He walked over to Win and Joe with his hand extended and a broad smile on his lips.

"Matthew Pate's the name, but folks call me Matt. You two boys are new around here, aren't you?"

"Just got off the train," Win said.

"Yes, I heard about the incident on the train with Mr. Tyrell." Matt took in the saloon with an expansive sweep of his long arm. "I own this place . . . and you are as welcome as rain. Especially after what you did for Christina.''

''Christina?''

''The girl you rescued on the train,'' Matt said.

''She works here?''

''In a manner of speaking, she does. She's my daughter,'' Matt said. He pointed toward the back of the saloon and there, coming down the stairs, was the same young woman Win had seen on the train. She smiled as she walked toward them.

''Hello,'' Christina said. ''We were not formally introduced on the train. I think my father told you, my name is Christina.''

''I'm Win.'' Win hesitated. He had removed the wanted poster, but someone might have seen it, and there might be others around. If so, the name Coulter would be recognized. He came up with another name. ''Carver. Win Carver. And this is my brother, Joe.''

''It is so nice to meet you,'' Christina said.

''Are you two boys staying in town?'' Matt asked.

''For a short time,'' Win said.

''Far as I'm concerned, you two can stay for as long as you want. But I have to warn you that you've made a dangerous enemy today. And he has dangerous friends.''

''Won't be the first time we've made enemies,'' Win replied.

Matt laughed. ''No, I'm sure it isn't.''

''Say, Matt, where might be a good place to eat around here?''

''I'd recommend Moynahan's, right next door,'' Matt answered. ''Tell you what. You two go over there and eat all you want. Tell Moynahan to put it on my tab.''

''That's mighty decent of you,'' Joe said. ''Win, what do you say we go have some supper? I could eat a horse.''

''Don't say that around Moynahan,'' Sandra teased,

coming back up to stand beside Joe. "You never know but what he might take you up on it."

Those close enough to overhear her laughed.

Joe looked at Sandra. "Will you be here when I come back?"

"Honey, in case you ain't noticed it, you've done got my comb red," Sandra said. "I'll be here waitin' for you, just anytime you're ready."

Sandra's directness caused Joe to take a quick breath.

"On second thought, Win, why don't you gone on over there without me?" he suggested.

"I thought you were so all-fired ready to have supper," Win said.

"Yeah, well, I've got somethin' else in mind right now."

"All right. I guess I can eat by myself."

"You don't have to eat by yourself, Mr. Carver," Christina said. "Unless you'd rather not be bothered with a foolish girl's company."

Win smiled. "Well, now, if I turned down the offer of such beautiful company, *I'd* be the fool," he said. "I would be pleased and honored to have you eat with me." He offered Christina his arm.

JOE WATCHED WIN AND CHRISTINA LEAVE THE SALOON, then turned his attention back to Sandra. "So, what do we do now?" he asked.

"I'm sure something will"—Sandra looked pointedly at the front of his pants—"come up," she said, emphasizing the last two words. Again, those who were close by laughed.

Sandra turned and started walking away, glancing back over her shoulder to let Joe know that she intended him to follow her. They went up the stairs and along the second-floor hallway. From his position behind her, Joe could watch her butt wiggle inside the snug fit of the red satin gown she was wearing.

"My room is down at the end of the hall," she said. "It's in the back so we won't be bothered by any noise from below."

"Honey, there are times when noise doesn't bother me," Joe replied. "And this is one of those times. We could be alongside the railroad track for all I care."

Sandra unlocked the door, then pushed it open, inviting Joe to go in first. The room, which was considerably larger than a normal hotel room, was dominated by a four-poster bed. The bed cover was a bright scarlet, and there were curtains to match hanging at the windows.

The windows on the back wall looked out onto a freight company, its yards busy with departing and arriving wagons. A large sign on top of the building read: "Bellefontaine Freight." Beyond it, the sun was setting in a blaze of gold and red.

"You just going to stand there and look at them wagons all day?" Sandra asked. "Or is there something I could do that might get you interested in me?"

When Joe turned back around, he saw her working on the buttons at the back of her gown. She watched him with smoky eyes and a provocative grin as she undid the last button and let the gown fall way to her waist, exposing her large breasts. She started pushing the gown down over her hips, squirming as she did so, causing her breasts to jiggle.

"You plannin' on doin' this with all your clothes on?" Sandra asked.

Joe grinned crookedly. "I guess it would be better if I shucked out of them," he said.

Joe was out of his clothes so quickly that Sandra barely had time to flip the scarlet coverlet back. Then they were in bed together, and without any further preliminaries, he moved on top of her as her legs went around his waist and her hands slid up from his ribs to grab him just below the shoulders.

Joe was propped on his hands and knees on the bed, so enjoying the sight of nakedness that he was almost unable to restrain himself. Reaching down, she helped him make the connection. Then he lunged, hot and hard, deep into her. He pulled back slowly and held himself for a second before thrusting into her again. After that, he established a steady pace of long, powerful thrusts and withdrawals.

He felt half drunk, his hips rocking in long slow thrusts, watching every thrust reverberate through her, her big breasts jiggling, erect nipples pointing up at him. He managed to keep himself just below climax, pacing himself so it would last, so he could bring her with him.

Joe felt Sandra's fingernails rake down across his ribs, saw her grin widen to a pleased leer as he jerked in response. He took her with him, right up to where he was, hanging on the edge, hot and blood pounding with lust.

Joe slid one arm under the small of her back, lifting her up from the bed until only her shoulders touched the sheet. He began thrusting deeper into her, long and slow and powerful, feeling that hot drunken lust raging through his brain, driving and driving into her until he saw her eyes close, saw her hands come down to clutch at the sheet, saw her head begin to rock from side to side, her lower lip caught between her teeth.

And then the little cries began to come from her; he felt her ankles lock across his back, her hands clutch the bed for leverage, and her hips pump frantically. For a moment he held her to a slower pace, never losing contact with her, until finally he let her go and felt her surge into wild rapid lunging.

Joe caught up to her pace, surpassed it, mastered it, then

mastered her, his own eyes closing from the heat of it. Through the blood pounding in his own ears he heard her wild cries as she surged up in a frantic rhythm that brought her up and over. He came after her, lunging and thrashing in a long final frenzy that brought them both back down on the bed. He felt her hands snake up around his neck, felt those big breasts heaving against his chest, felt her shudder up against him, shudder down again, and then leech herself to him in one final prolonged quiver, all her sleek round curves soft against his skin.

They lay that way for what seemed like a long time, on their sides, her head tucked down under his. He was still in the warm hollow of her thighs, her legs around his waist. He cupped the nape of her neck, feeling consciousness slowly returning. A faint breeze stirred curtains at the open window. By now the sun had set and there was only the final crimson glow in the west. The clatter of wagons and the activity had stilled at the freight yard, the day's work of the many employees completed.

"I've been with my share of men," Sandra finally said, breaking the silence. "But it's not often I lose myself like that." She grinned and slid a sharp fingernail up his chest. "A fella like you could make me forget I'm even in the business. This one is on the house."

Joe laughed, then shook his head. "Uh-uh," he said. "When I get my money's worth of anything, I expect to pay for it." He reached for his pants. "And darlin', you gave me my money's worth."

"Too bad you can't take advantage of a special offer I have," Sandra said.

"Now, what offer would that be?"

"My two-for-one sale."

Joe put the money on a bedside table, then smiled at her.

"And just what makes you think I can't take advantage of it?" he asked, moving down to take one of her nipples into his mouth.

"Oh, my," Sandra said, feeling him growing again. "You *are* quite a man!"

THE CHINA, SILVER, AND CRYSTAL GLEAMED SOFTLY IN the reflected light of more than a dozen lanterns. Moynahan's Restaurant was an oasis of light in the darkness that had descended over the little town.

"The Bellefontaine ranch takes up most of the county," Christina was explaining as she ate with Win. "Bellefontaine Ranch is now made up of what used to be Trailback, the Lazy M, Doubletree, and a couple of other, smaller ranches. I was born on Doubletree. It belonged to my father."

"I didn't realize your father was a rancher."

"He was a rancher and so was my grandfather before him. When Bellefontaine took over Doubletree, he got a ranch that had been thriving since Texas was part of Mexico."

"I don't understand. If the ranch was doing that well, why did you father sell out to Bellefontaine?"

Christina looked up sharply. "My father didn't sell Doubletree," she said. "He had it stolen from him. Not one penny did he get for it."

"How can that be?"

"Bellefontaine got Doubletree the same way he got Trailback and all the other ranches. He paid the taxes and took over the property. Only in my father's case, he didn't even know there were any taxes due. Bellefontaine took the taxes off the books and paid them before the notices were even sent out."

"But how could he get away with something like that?" Win asked. "Where was the law?"

"Bellefontaine *is* the law. You have to remember that none of our officials actually represent the people now. They have all been appointed to their positions by the people in Washington. We lost the war, Mr. Carver, and the Yankees are seeing to it that we pay for it."

"I ran across the constable when I came into town," Win said. "Charley Gibson, I think he said his name was. He mentioned that he used to be the sheriff."

Christina smiled. "Uncle Charley was sheriff for fifteen years."

"Uncle Charley?"

"My mother's brother," Christina explained. "He found out what Bellefontaine was doing with the taxes, and he started going around the county warning people. Bellefontaine got wind of it, and had the Yankees push Uncle Charley out of office."

"I believe he told me he wouldn't take the loyalty oath," Win said.

Christina smiled. "Bellefontaine knew that he would never take the oath, and he knew that was all it would take to get rid of him. So he had his cronies come down here and make Uncle Charley an offer. Either take the oath and help in the administration of the law, which meant evict people from the homes and ranches they and their parents before them had built, or refuse to take the oath and give up the office. Uncle Charley chose to give up the office, but I wish he would have taken it. The whole county was a lot better off when he was sheriff."

"He can't help anyone as constable?"

Christina shook her head. "He has no authority to do anything. Bellefontaine's hand-picked sheriff stops him every time he tries."

"That's him, right over there," a loud voice suddenly said.

Win looked toward the front door and saw Tim Tyrell pointing at him. The man Tyrell was talking to was a tall, broad-shouldered man with a sweeping handlebar mustache. He was wearing a badge.

"Is that the sheriff?" Win asked.

"Sheriff Angus Buford," Christina said.

"Buford?"

"Yes. Have you heard of him?"

"Yes, I have," Win said.

WHEN WIN AND THE OTHERS ARRIVED AT THE RUSSELL *farm, they found Mrs. Russell and her daughter standing on a rock. The women had their ankles tied together, and their wrists tied behind them. They each had a noose around their neck, and the noose was tied to a tree limb overhead. If either of them slipped, or fell off the rock, they would be stepping into eternity.*

From another limb, hanging so that the women could clearly see them, were the bodies of Mr. Russell and his two sons, one of whom was only fifteen. The men had been hanged the day before, and the two women had remained tied on the rock, poised one half-step from death, for nearly twenty-four hours when Win arrived.

"Cut the women down!" Win ordered quickly. Both women collapsed from exhaustion, and it wasn't until after the men had been buried that they were recovered enough to tell what had happened.

"It was Jayhawkers," Mrs. Russell said.

"Do you know who?" Win asked.

"I heard 'em call out his name," the girl answered. "It was Buford. Don't know iffen that was his first name or his last, but Buford it was."

•   •   •

"I DON'T KNOW WHAT YOU HAVE HEARD ABOUT HIM,"
Christina said quietly. "But I can tell you this. He's as
mean a man as ever kicked a dog."

4

ALL EYES IN THE RESTAURANT WERE ON THE SHERIFF AS he walked over to the table where Win and Christina were eating. Win got up from the table and wiped his mouth with a napkin before he turned toward the sheriff. It was a casual move, but one that cleared the way for Win to pull his gun quickly if need be. The move wasn't lost on Buford, who halted for just a step or two before continuing on.

"Something I can do for you, Sheriff?" Win asked.

"What's your name?" the sheriff asked.

"My name is Win Carver." Win smiled disarmingly. "And you must be the Sheriff Buford I've heard so much about."

Buford stroked his chin with his forefinger. "You look familiar to me, Mr. Carver. We ever run acrost each other afore?"

"I doubt it. I just arrived in town today."

"Wasn't talkin' about here. I was talkin' about before," Buford said.

"Could be," Win answered. "I've traveled around quite a bit since the war. I figure you have too, seein' as that's no Texas accent."

"Kansas," Buford answered. "And yours is what? Missouri?"

Win smiled. "Arkansas, but folks often get us confused. I reckon it's them Ozark hills. Makes us all sound the same."

Buford nodded toward Tyrell, who hadn't advanced beyond the door. "This fella says you pushed him off the train. Did you?"

"No."

"What?" Tyrell shouted, his voice practically going into falsetto. "Sheriff Buford, he's lying!"

Buford stroked his chin again, and studied Win for a moment. "Now, let me get this straight. You're saying you did *not* push Tim Tyrell off the train?"

"That's what I'm saying."

"Look at him. He's bruised and cut, his clothes are dirty and torn. How do you reckon he got that way?"

"I think it happened when he fell off," Win said. "I saw him fall. I reached out to grab him, but it was too late." Win smiled. "Now that I think about it, he must've seen me reach for him." Win smiled broadly. "Why, Sheriff, I'll just bet that's why he thinks I pushed him."

"You *did* push me!"

"Mr. Carver is telling the truth, Sheriff," Christina said. "I was on the train too, and I saw the whole thing."

"You're lying! Both of you!" Tyrell sputtered in frustrated anger.

"Tyrell," Win said coldly. "I'd think twice about calling a lady a liar if I were you."

"Carver, I don't intend to let you start anything in here," Buford said quickly.

"I'm not planning on starting anything, Sheriff," Win said. "But I'll damn sure finish it."

Buford looked at Win for a long moment, then turned to

Tyrell. "Tyrell, it looks to me like you fell off the train. Try and be more careful from now on."

"But . . ." Tyrell said.

"Go on back to the ranch," the sheriff told him. "If you stay in town you're going to get yourself in trouble."

Defeated, Tyrell turned and left the restaurant.

Buford went with him, but just before he exited, he stopped long enough to let his eyes sweep around the room, taking in all the diners, as if making a mental note for future reference as to who was there.

Buford's exit was followed by a collective sigh of relief from all. Then there was a sudden buzz of excited voices as everyone trying to talk at once. Whatever the subjects of conversation had been before Sheriff Buford came into the room, they had all changed. Now everyone was talking about what they had just seen.

"Thanks for backing me up," Win said to Christina. "Under the circumstances, lying seemed the best way to go." He laughed. "And you have to admit, my denying it did about give Mr. Tyrell conniptions."

Christina put her hand across the table and rested it on Win's arm. "Watch out for Sheriff Buford, Win," she said. "He is not the kind you would want to turn your back on."

"Thanks for the warning," Win said.

AT THAT SAME MOMENT, IN THE DARK STREET JUST IN front of the restaurant, Tyrell and Sheriff Buford were talking.

"I can't believe you let the son of a bitch get away with lying like that," Tyrell growled. "You should've done something about it."

"What could I do about it? The girl backed him up."

"She was lying too."

"She said it in front of the entire restaurant," Buford

said. "Even if I had arrested him, when it came to a court hearing, it would be their word against yours."

"I thought you had some loyalty to General Bellefontaine."

"I've proved my loyalty to the general many times," Buford said. "I don't have to prove it to you."

"Sergeant Buford, you forget I was a lieutenant and—"

"It's *Sheriff* Buford now, Tyrell. And I haven't forgotten anything. I had to go along with it during the war 'cause you was duly appointed over me—and because you are the general's nephew. But the war's over and you don't outrank me anymore. In fact, you ain't jack-shit now, and I don't intend to waste my time wiping the snot off your nose ever' time you bite off more'n you can chew."

"If you're talkin' about that bushwhacker I got into it with the other night, I coulda handled him. I didn't ask you to arrest him."

"You could've handled him? He was half an inch away from killin' you. It's a good thing we're hangin' him tomorrow. Otherwise he'd be comin' after you."

"All right, so maybe I did let the argument get a little out of hand. At least I got him to admit that he was a bushwhacker, didn't I? I mean, if he hadn't started braggin' about ridin' with Quantrill, you woulda never known."

"That's right. I would've never known."

"So, now, what about Carver? What are you going to do about him?"

"I'm not going to do anything about him."

"Sergeant, you can't just—" Tyrell began but Buford held up his index finger and shook it back and forth. "I mean, Sheriff," Tyrell said. "You can't just do nothing."

"The hell I can't. If you have a problem with Carver, take care of it yourself."

"All right," Tyrell said. His eyes narrowed. "All right,

I will. But when it happens, you just remember that it was your idea.''

"When what happens?" Buford scoffed as he mounted his horse. "Carver would shoot you down before you even cleared leather."

"How do you know?"

"Because I know Carver."

"You know him?"

"Not him personally, but I know his kind. His soul died during the war. What's left is nothing but pure hate and venom. His kind is going to kill until he gets killed, and it don't matter that much to him which way it comes out.'' Buford clucked at his horse and began to ride away.

"Yeah, well, he doesn't look so tough to me!" Tyrell called after him. "You just watch me and see! I'll handle him!"

Tyrell looked back toward Moynahan's Restaurant. Carver had now made a fool of him three times. Once on the train, once in the saloon, and once in the restaurant. Three times! He was not going to let that happen again. Whatever it took, he was going to make things right with Mr. Win Carver. He looked down the dark street toward Buford. "And when I settle with Mr. Carver, I may just have an accounting with *you*," he said under his breath.

WIN AND CHRISTINA HAD JUST FINISHED EATING, AND were about to leave the restaurant, when Joe came in.

"So, how was supper?" Joe asked, his words jaunty, his mood ebullient.

"Well, Little Brother, you certainly look bright-eyed and bushy-tailed."

"Do I? Well, a little lady named Sandra and I had some very pleasant business to attend to."

"So it appears. I'm glad to see that you decided to take the time to eat," Win teased.

"Believe me, after what I've just been through, I need to eat," he said. "I have to get my strength back."

Christina laughed, and Joe suddenly realized that he had said more than he intended. He smiled sheepishly, and put his hand to the brim of his hat. "Beg your pardon, ma'am," he said. "I sure hope I didn't give offense."

"You don't have to apologize to me," Christina said. "From what I have heard, Sandra can be a most energetic woman."

"Yes, ma'am, I'll vouch for that," Joe said. Then he asked Win, "Are you leaving?"

"Yes. I'm going to walk Christina back. Then I'll get us a room at the hotel. Unless you've made other plans," he added pointedly.

"Sandra offered, but I need my rest," Joe quipped.

"And you were the one complaining about having to stay here," Win teased. "Try the steak, it's very good."

"Reckon I'll just try two steaks," Joe replied.

Win laughed, then held the door open for Christina as they went outside.

"You and your brother seem to get along very well," she said.

"Yes."

"That's good. I think family should be close. What about the rest of your family? Any other brothers, sisters? Where do you parents live?"

"Joe and I are all that's left," Win said. "Our mother and father were killed during the war. Jayhawkers."

Christina put her hand on Win's arm. "Oh, Win, I'm sorry," she said.

"It was several years ago. I don't think about it much

anymore," Win lied, recalling the dream he had on the train.

THE TOWN OF SAN SABA WAS ACTUALLY TWO TOWNS, DIvided by the railroad track. The north side of the track was the American side, while the Mexican population was concentrated on the south side.

Rip-sawed lumber buildings made up the American town, while across the tracks, adobe buildings were laid out around a dusty plaza.

Tim Tyrell crossed over to the south side of the tracks, then tied his horse off at a hitch rail in front of Jose's Cantina. A woman's high, clear voice was singing, and it and the accompanying guitar music spilled out through the beaded doorway.

Although Tyrell knew that the Mexicans were generally much poorer than the Americans, you couldn't tell that by listening. The cantina was buzzing with energetic conversation, and bubbling over with laughter.

Tyrell pushed through the hanging beads. He was sure he could find a solution to his problem inside.

CHRISTINA AND HER FATHER LIVED ON THE TOP FLOOR OF the saloon, and it was a walk of no more than a few dozen steps from the restaurant to Matt's Place. Win escorted her home, then told her good-bye and started down the street to the hotel to get a room for himself and his brother.

It was very dark outside. There were no street lamps in this small town, so that only the moon and a few dim squares of light splashing through open windows kept it from being as black as the inside of a pit. At the far end of the street, however, Win could see the gruesome shape of the gallows. It was dimly lighted by the moon, and by a splash of light which fell from the front window of the jail house.

The piano player, who had been absent when Win was in the saloon earlier, was hard at work now, an empty beer mug sitting on top of the piano in the hope that there would be a few generous patrons. Now his rendition of ''Lorena'' spilled out into the street from Matt's Place.

From the shadows of the Mexican quarters on the south side of the tracks Win could hear a guitar and trumpet. They were playing different songs, yet somehow it all seemed to blend into a single melody.

A dog barked.

Somewhere a baby cried.

Win saw the lights of the hotel and started toward them.

He felt the assassins coming for him before he heard them, and he heard them before he saw them. Two men suddenly jumped from the dark shadows between the buildings, making wide slashes with their knives. Only that innate sense which allowed him to perceive danger when there was no other sign saved his life, for he was moving out of the way at the exact moment the two men were starting their attacks. Otherwise their knives, swinging in low, vicious arcs, would have disemboweled him.

Despite the quickness of his reaction, however, one of the knives did manage to cut him, and as Win went down into the dirt, rolling to get away from them, the flashing blade opened up a long wound in his side. The knife was so sharp and wielded so adroitly that Win barely felt it. He knew, however, that the knife had drawn blood.

But for all their skill with the blades, the assassins had made a bad mistake. Both were wearing white *peon* shirts and trousers, so that despite the darkness of the street they were easy to see, and being easy to see, were easy to avoid. One of the assassins moved in quickly, thinking to finish

Win off before he could recover. But Win twisted around on the ground, then thrust his feet out, catching the assailant in the chest with a powerful kick and driving him back several feet. The other one darted in then, his action keeping Win off his feet and away from his gun.

The assailants were good, skilled and agile. Win sent a booted foot whistling toward one of them, catching the man in the groin. Then he lunged upward, and rammed stiff fingers to gouge the other in both eyes.

"Aiiyee!" the assailant screamed, dropping his knife and reaching up to his face.

The one who had been kicked in the groin reached for his partner and, pulling him away, broke off the fight. The two men ran toward the track, then disappeared into the darkness on the other side before Win managed to get a good look at their faces. He knew only that they were Mexicans, but he didn't know why they had attacked him.

Win felt the nausea beginning to rise. Bile surged to his throat. Light-headed now, he turned and staggered back down the road toward the saloon. He grabbed the porch pillar for support and pulled himself up onto the plank porch, then pushed in through the door to stand in the brightness.

One of the bar girls happened to be looking toward the door just as he came in, and seeing the bloody apparition standing there, screamed.

All conversation stopped at Win's entrance, and a dead silence hung over the saloon as if it were something palpable. Everyone stared at him, their eyes wide and their mouths open in shock.

Win didn't realize it, but he was terrifying to behold. He was standing just inside the doorway, ashen-faced and holding his hand over a wound which spilled bright red blood between his fingers. With a silly, disconnected grin on his face, he surveyed the room for just a moment, then with effort, walked over to the bar.

''Whiskey,'' he ordered.

The solemn-faced bartender poured him a glass and Win took it, then turned around to face the silent patrons. By now his side was drenched with blood from his wound, and the blood was beginning to soak into the wide-plank floor.

''Win!'' Christina shouted in alarm. She had gone up to her room when he brought her home, and now she hurried back down the stairs and ran over to him.

''Hello, Christina,'' Win said. He smiled and held his glass out toward her, offering a toast. Then his eyes rolled back in his head and he crumpled to the floor, passed out cold.

5

"IN HERE," CHRISTINA SAID. "WE WILL PUT HIM IN MY room."

Joe had been quickly summoned from the restaurant next door, and now he was carrying his brother in his arms. He pushed through the door into Christina's room.

The room was hot and humid, and Christina and Joe could smell the blood from Win's wound. Christina felt around in the dark until she found the bedside table and candle. A moment later she found the box of lucifers and struck one, then held the flame to the candle until a small light perched atop the taper. The dark of the room was pushed away.

"Put him on my bed."

Joe hesitated for a moment. "Do you have any towels or anything to put down? He'll be upset if he finds out he bled on your bed."

"I have an old blanket we can use," Christina offered, getting one from the bottom drawer of the bureau, then spreading it out on her bed.

Joe laid his brother down gingerly. "Did you see who did this to him?" he asked.

"No, but some men in the saloon saw them. They said it was a couple of Mexicans from the other side of town," Christina said.

"Why would a couple of Mexicans attack Win?" Joe asked. "We ain't done nothin' to none of them."

"Robbery, perhaps?" Christina suggested.

"He doesn't have that much money. And believe me, there's easier ways to make money than tryin' to steal from Win. What about that little pissant Tyrell? Does he know any Mexicans? Maybe he hired 'em."

"That's very possible," Christina said. "There are many Mexicans on the other side of the track who would do anything if the price is right," Christina said. "And I'm sure Mr. Tyrell would be acquainted with such people."

"Yeah, well, if you ask me, Tyrell hired them Mexicans to cut up Win, sure as a gun is iron. Only the Mexicans didn't know what they was gettin' themselves in to, or like as not they wouldn't of done it."

"Two men attacking him in the dark with knives," Christina said. "He is lucky he wasn't killed."

Joe looked down at his brother. "Yeah, he has bled a lot, hasn't he? You think I should get a doctor?"

Christina shook his head. "There is no doctor in San Saba. The nearest one is fifty miles away. But I sometimes help the doctor when he is here, so I know how to treat the wound. Also, I've got some salve, crushed aloe leaves, and plenty of fresh wrappings for bandages. I would be glad to take care of him."

"I appreciate that," Joe said. "And if you don't mind, I'll just leave him with you until I can get us a room over at the hotel." Joe started to leave, then stopped just before he stepped through the door and looked back toward Christina. "You think I should come back later tonight?"

"No, that won't be necessary," Christina said. "Or even

desired. Once I get him bandaged, he will need get a good night's sleep.'' She smiled. ''You could probably use a little rest as well. Go on over to the hotel. If I need you, I'll send someone for you, I promise.''

''All right, whatever you say,'' Joe agreed.

WHEN CHRISTINA SAT ON THE BED BESIDE WIN A FEW moments later, his eyes snapped open. He saw her reach down to loosen his belt and start unfastening the buttons on his pants.

''What?'' Win asked. He tried to sit up. ''What are you doing?''

''Shh, lie back down,'' Christina said quietly. She pushed him back down gently. ''I'm trying to help you,'' she said.

Slowly, Christina began peeling the blood-soaked clothes away from his skin to expose his wound. ''I'm going to treat your cut. Then I'm going to wash your clothes.''

''You don't have to worry about that. I hate to be a bother. I'll be all right,'' Win insisted.

''No, you won't be all right unless the wound is cleaned and treated. And you can't walk around wearing blood-soaked clothes,'' she said. ''I have soap and water for your clothes and medicines for you, so I may as well take care of it.''

She took off his shirt, then removed his pants, though for the time being she protected his modesty by the strategic placement of a towel.

Christina sucked in her breath as she looked at the cut and the blood which had coagulated around the wound. ''You have lost quite a bit of blood. It is no wonder you passed out.''

''Did I pass out?''

"Yes, of course you did. Do you mean you don't remember?"

"No," Win said. "I remember the fight, and I remember coming into the saloon. Then I don't remember another thing until I woke up just a moment ago."

Christina chuckled. "What do you call that, if it isn't passing out?"

"I guess I would call it going to sleep real fast," Win joked. He laughed, then winced as a stab of pain cut through his side.

"You must be still now," Christina instructed. She got up from the bed, then walked over to the bureau to pour water from a porcelain pitcher into a basin.

Win lay back and folded his hands behind his head. The muscles in his arms, shoulders, and chest rippled as he did so, and he watched as the beautiful young woman poured the water, then brought it back over to set it on the small bedside table. Again she sat on the bed beside him.

Gently, she began cleaning the blood from Win's side. The knife wound started just above the belt line, then disappeared below the towel she had put on him. Christina slipped the towel a little farther down. His pubic hair, which began as a tiny dark line at his navel, broadened into a dark, curling bush. As the entire length of the cut was now visible, she stopped before any more of his privacy was compromised.

"It doesn't appear to be too deep," she said as she examined the cut critically. "And I don't think any of the vital organs inside were cut."

Win looked directly into her eyes, and saw the latent smoke of lust in their depths.

For reasons she couldn't explain, Christina felt a tremendous heat suffusing her body as she cleaned his wound. She felt his abdomen. It was incredibly hot, perhaps fevered by the wound, yet she could feel the pulsing of his blood just beneath the skin. Though it wasn't necessary for her to pull the towel any farther down, she couldn't stop herself from doing so, now exposing him to her.

When his wound was completely clean she applied a salve to it, then began to rub the crushed medicinal herbs on it.

"Does it feel good?" she asked.

"Yeah," Win croaked.

Even though she had completed applying the medication, she let her hand continue to rub his skin, as if mesmerized by it. Her hand moved in ever-widening circles until finally it reached his penis. Then, as if moving of its own volition, her fingers wrapped around it, squeezing it until it began to grow in her hands.

"That feels good too," Win croaked. He reached up to feel her breast through her dress.

"Wait," she said. She walked over to her door, opened it, looked outside, then closed and locked it. When she returned to the bed she began removing her dress. She laid it neatly on a chair, its colors visible by candlelight, then stepped out of her petticoat. Next came the camisole, followed by her bloomers. That left her as naked as he was.

Hesitating for a moment, as if either unsure of what to do next or frightened to proceed any further, Christina just stood by the bed for a moment, displaying her young, beautiful body to him. Her nipples glowed softly, while shadows kept mysterious the promise of her thighs. Then, drawing a deep breath and gathering her courage, she sat back down on the bed and looked at him.

Win raised his hand to one of her nipples, and it hardened under his touch. He tried to sit up, winced in pain, then lay back down.

"You are wounded," she said. "You might not be able to do this."

"We'll find a way," Win insisted.

"Yes," Christina agreed. "We'll find a way." She leaned down and kissed his neck, then started working her way down his chest. Win could feel the soft velvet heat of her darting tongue as she licked his skin, trailing back and forth until she stopped at his nipple and flicked her tongue over it several times. Win tried to move over her, but again the pain stabbed at him. When Christina saw that, she smiled gently and put her cool fingers on his shoulders to indicate that he should stay where he was.

"You just lie there. I'll take care of everything," she said.

"You're the doctor," Win teased.

Studying him closely through lust-filled eyes, Christina moved over him, straddling him, preparing to take him into her, orchestrating the moment for both of them. She reached down to grab Win's steel-hard penis, then put the head of it just inside her slick, wet crack, and pulled it in.

She sat down on it, and Win watched as his cock pushed into her, like a lubricated piston sliding into a cylinder. He raised his hips to facilitate the move.

The bedsprings began to creak, and Christina whimpered and moaned in her rapture as she made love to him. Win felt bubbles of fire ascending from his belly up through what connected them together, and he felt her jerk in wild spasms as the jolts of rapture racked her body. Then Win felt her slacken above him, and he put his hands on her hips to hold her down to him as, with a groan, she fell across him even as he was spending himself inside her in his final, convulsive shudders.

They remained that way for several moments, with Christina lying on top, allowing the heat and the pleasure to drain slowly from her body. Finally she disconnected from him, his penis making a tiny sucking sound as she pulled herself from it. Then she stood beside the bed and looked down at him. Her tongue slid out of her mouth to lick across her lips.

"You are the first man I have been with since my husband," she said.

"Your husband?" Win replied in a shocked voice. Almost without thinking, he raised himself to his elbows and looked toward the door. "I didn't know you were married."

"I'm a widow," Christina said quickly. She chuckled softly. "Did you think you were going to see him coming through the door?"

"I gave it a passing thought," Win admitted sheepishly. "What happened to your husband?"

"He was a lieutenant in my father's company. They were both part of General Kirby Smith's division. Johnny Rawlings was killed at the Battle of Palmetto Ranch on the Rio Grande."

"Palmetto Ranch? I've heard of that battle. It took place after Lee surrendered at Appomattox. It was even after Jefferson Davis was captured."

"Yes," Christina said. "It was the last battle of the war."

"That was every soldier's worst nightmare, you know," Win said. "To get killed by the last bullet in the last fight of the war."

"And every wife and mother's nightmare as well," Christina said. She began to get dressed then. "My father says that we won that battle. But the fact that we won the battle seemed little consolation when they unloaded Johnny's body from the train. And now I can't even visit his grave, for he was buried in the family cemetery at Doubletree. Johnny, my mother, my baby sister, my grandparents. They are all buried on land that now belongs to Jason Bellefontaine, and he won't even let us visit their graves.''

"I'm sorry," Win said.

Christina looked at him and smiled wanly. "No, I am the one who should be sorry," she said. "It was wrong of me to bring all of this up, especially after what we just did."

"No, it was good for you to bring it up. I think you needed to talk about it," Win said. "And if it helped, I'm glad I was here."

Christina looked down at his wound and saw that it was bleeding again, though not as badly as before.

"I'm going to have to redo the bandage. We've opened your wound again. We should have been more careful. I shouldn't have been so . . . so aggressive."

Win smiled. "It doesn't hurt at all," he said. "And you weren't aggressive, you were generous. Believe me, it was worth it."

6

WHEN WIN AWAKENED THE NEXT MORNING, HE EXPERIenced a moment of confusion about where he was. But when he moved, a sharp stitch in his side reminded him of what had happened the night before, and he reached down to feel the bandage. He was gratified to see that there had been no more bleeding since the previous night.

Win looked around at his surroundings. He knew that he was in Christina's room, but it had been dark when he was brought here, and he hadn't been able to see much.

He didn't know exactly what time it was, but he could tell by the texture of the sunlight streaming in through the window that it was still fairly early in the morning. He also saw his clothes, clean and nearly dry, spread out near the window to take advantage of the warm air and sun.

He lay back in bed for a few more moments, listening to the sounds of a town coming to grips with a new day.

The first sound to get his attention was a heavy, thumping sound. For a moment he didn't recognize it. Then, with a chill, he realized what it had to be. Down at the far end of the street the workers on the hangman's gallows were testing the trapdoor. They were letting it fall open, time and time again. Each successful triggering of the trapdoor was marked with a heavy, rattling thump.

Thump.

Thump.

Thump.

From the blacksmith shop he could hear the sound of the smithy shaping a piece of iron at his forge. The hammer made a ringing sound on the off-beat of the thumping trap door.

Thump.

Ring.

Thump.

Ring.

Thump.

Ring.

Downstairs, the bartender was sweeping off the front porch of the saloon, and he added the scratch of his broom to the thump of the door and the ring of the hammer. Though unintended, the result was a rhythmic composition.

Thump, ring, scratch-scratch-scratch . . . Thump, ring, scratch-scratch-scratch.

There were other sounds as well: the hollow clop of hooves on the sunbaked dirt of the street, the rattle of a freight wagon coming slowly into town. Some children were playing a game of hide-and-seek, and a nearby sign creaked as it moved back and forth in the morning breeze.

The door to his room opened then, and Joe came in, carrying Win's breakfast on a tray.

"How do you feel?" Joe asked.

Win sat up, pleasantly surprised to see that moving wasn't that difficult an ordeal.

"I'm a little sore," he admitted, putting his hand over the bandage to test his wound. "But Christina did a pretty good job of patching me up. I think I'm all right."

"Good. Speaking of Christina, I saw that she was about to bring your breakfast to you, but I told her she didn't have to do that. I figured you would rather have me bring it."

"Oh, hell, yes, of course I would rather you bring it. I would much rather look at your ugly face than see her again," Win teased as he picked up a piece of bacon from the plate.

"Yeah, well, I had a reason for wanting to see you alone," Joe said.

"It better be a good one." He broke off a piece of biscuit and raked it through the yellow of his fried egg.

Joe held up his finger as if asking Win to wait a minute. Then he stepped to the doorway and looked up and down the hallway to make certain no one was standing just outside, before he closed the door.

Win laughed because he had seen Christina do the same thing last night, just before she took off her clothes.

"What is it?" Joe asked, a confused expression on his face. "Why did you laugh?"

Win shook his head. "Never mind," he said around a full mouth. "It was just something I thought of, that's all. I don't think it would interest you."

"That's all right. I have something that will definitely interest you," Joe said.

"What?"

"I went by to visit Ray this morning."

"In jail?"

"Yes."

"Wasn't that a little risky?"

"I told Gibson that I knew some of the men who rode for Quantrill, and I wanted to ask his prisoner about them. Gibson didn't question me at all. In fact, he even left the jail while I was there so Ray and I could talk alone for a few minutes.''

"How is Ray holding out?"

"He's pretty nervous about it," Joe said. "He doesn't want to hang."

"Can't say as I blame him. Don't reckon anyone would feel too good in that position."

"Win, do you know why he asked us here?"

"It was supposed to have something to do with money."

"It does have to do with money. Lots of it," Joe replied.

"How much money? And how do we get to it?"

Joe chuckled. "Well, now, that's the problem," he said.

"What do you mean?"

"Ray say's he ain't goin' to tell us anything more about it until tomorrow."

"Tomorrow? Hell, what's he talkin' about? There ain't goin' to be a tomorrow for him. They're plannin' on hangin' 'im today, aren't they?"

"That's his point, Win. If we want to find out what this is all about, we're goin' to have to get him out of the pickle he's in."

"What did you tell him?"

"I told him don't worry about it, you are a pretty smart fella, you can come up with something," Joe said. He rubbed his hands together and smiled broadly. "So, have you got any ideas?"

"Why do I have to have all the ideas?"

" 'Cause you're the smart one, I'm the good-lookin' one," Joe said with a wide grin. "Ma always said so."

"Yeah, well . . ." Win paused and looked at his brother, then laughed. "Ma was half right. All right, I'll come up with something. But you're going to have to help me on with my boots," Win said.

"Help you with your boots? Why the hell do I have to help you with your boots?"

Win pushed the rest of his breakfast away. " 'Cause we aren't going to be able to stop the hangin' with me layin' in bed."

"All right," Joe said, looking around the room. "I'll help you with your boots."

IT WAS JUST AFTER NOON, AND WIN AND JOE WERE STANDING in the alley behind the livery stable.

"Here are the wood shavings you asked for," Joe said, setting a bag down in front of Win. "I got 'em from a pile out behind the cabinet shop."

A couple of horses in the lot whickered, and Win looked around to make certain no one was coming. When he was sure they weren't being watched, he emptied a whole can of kerosene into the sack of wood shavings, then stirred them around so that all of them were wet. After that, he took a piece of rawhide and tied it around the bottom of Joe's right trouser leg so that the cord would hold the pants cuff in a blouse, tight against the boot.

"I still don't know why I'm the one has to do this," Joe said.

"Because I'm the one who came up with the idea," Win reminded him. "Now, loosen your belt and pull your trouser waist out," Win ordered.

"Just because you—"

Joe's comment was interrupted when Win, suddenly and unceremoniously, dumped the entire sack of shavings down into his pants.

"Hey! What the hell?"

"Push those shavings on down your right pants leg," Win ordered.

"Win, have you gone crazy?"

"You don't want my hand poking around down there, do you, Little Brother?"

"You stick your hand down there and I'll break it off at the elbow," Joe growled as he began directing the shavings down his right leg. "These damned things itch," he complained.

"You won't have to put up with them too long," Win promised.

IT WAS ABOUT ONE-THIRTY WHEN JOE WALKED, A LITTLE stiff-leggedly, down to the gallows. There was still half an hour before the scheduled hanging, but the crowd was already thick, filling the street from porch to porch, jostling for position. Although individually most in the crowd thought that the hanging was an unjust penalty for someone who had done nothing more than ride with Quantrill during the war, there was nevertheless a festive air to the crowd. The celebration came from the fact that a hanging was a spectator event of the first order.

The crowd was made up of a cross section of the town. Standing unobtrusively at the rear of the crowd were a score or more of Mexican men, wearing peasant shirts, colorful serapes, and wide, fringe-brimmed sombreros.

Nearby, an old Mexican woman was selling tortillas from a box she carried. She didn't have any teeth, and she kept her mouth closed so tightly that her chin and nose nearly touched. A swarm of flies buzzed around the box, drawn by the pungent aromas of beans and sauces. She worked with quick, deft fingers, rolling the spicy ingredients into tortillas, then handing them to her customers.

The Americans, many of whom were the old woman's customers, were variously dressed in suits, shirtsleeves, and overalls; the women wore long dresses and bonnets and watched over the children, who threaded in and out of the groups as they chased one another, laughing at their games.

To one side of the crowd, on the opposite side of the street from the jail, a black-frocked preacher stood on an overturned box, taking advantage of the gathering to deliver a fiery sermon. The man was of average height and build, with a full head of thick black hair. Standing on the box, he jabbed his finger repeatedly toward the gallows as he harangued the crowd.

"In a few moments, a poor, miserable sinner is going to be hurled to eternity . . . sent to meet his Maker with blood on his hands and sin in his heart."

Several of the Mexicans, upon hearing that, crossed themselves and mouthed a quick prayer.

"No such thing, Preacher! That fella rode with Quantrill and he didn't do nothin' more'n kill a few Yankees!" someone shouted.

"He didn't kill enough of 'em, is my way of thinkin'," another added, and the crowd laughed and cheered the hecklers.

"Hell, yes! Instead of hangin' him, we ought to elect him to Congress!"

"Congress wouldn't take 'im! He ain't a big enough sinner!"

There was more laughter.

Undaunted, the preacher continued his sermon. He waggled his finger at the crowd. "Brothers and sisters, hear this now! That sinner is goin' to be cast into Hell because he has not repented of his sins!"

"Good for him!"

"Tell him to give the Devil a kick in the ass from me!"

There was more nervous laughter.

"It's too late for him, brothers and sisters! It's too late to save his soul, and he is consigned to the fiery furnace of Hell, doomed to writhe in agony forever!"

Again, the Mexicans crossed themselves, and now, even among the Americans in the crowd, the preacher's words began to sink in. A few shivered involuntarily at the powerful imagery of burning forever. One or two of them touched their necks fearfully, and a few souls, perhaps weak on willpower, sneaked a drink from a bottle.

"It's too late for them, but it's not too late for you! Repent! Repent now, I say, for the wages of sin are death and eternal damnation!"

Joe moved quietly and unobserved through the crowd. The preacher had everyone's attention, which was exactly what he needed. With a lit cigar in his mouth, he moved over to stand directly adjacent to the foot of the gallows, where a pile of sawdust and wood shavings remained from the recent construction.

Joe reached down with his knife and cut the rawhide cord that had bloused his trouser leg. Then he shook the pants leg to allow the coal-oil-soaked shavings to fall out of the bottom of his pants. That done, he took several more puffs on the cigar to get the tip glowing brightly, then dropped the cigar in the pile of shavings.

It took but a moment for the shavings to flame up. As soon as Joe saw that the fire had caught, he moved back into the crowd, edging over to the opening between the jailhouse and the hardware store.

"After this here hangin' takes place," the preacher was saying, "I invite all of you to come down to the creek with me! Come down to the creek and get right with God! Ask Him to save your souls from eternal perdition and I will dunk you in His cleansing waters! I will. . . . *Holy shit!*" the preacher suddenly shouted.

"What'd you say, Preacher?" somebody in the crowd asked, shocked by the preacher's outburst.

"Fire!" the preacher shouted, pointing to the gallows. "The goddamned gallows is on fire!"

The crowd turned to see what the preacher was talking about, and they saw flames shooting up the side of the gallows, licking over onto the gallows floor, and leaping up to the cross-beam where the rope, already in place, was also burning.

The women screamed and the men swore. Sheriff Buford and his deputies, the hangman, and Constable Gibson all ran out of the jailhouse to see what was going on.

"Goddamn! How did this happen? Buckets! Get the buckets!" Buford shouted in agitation.

Mothers began calling for their children as several men ran to get buckets to extinguish the flames. In all the confusion, no one saw Joe moving quickly through the narrow passageway between the jail and the hardware store.

In the alley behind the hardware store, three saddled horses were tied. Joe untied them, mounted one, then held the reins of the other two, keeping them ready.

Sixty feet away Win started running back toward the horses. Behind Win, against the back wall of the jail, a little string of smoke began working up from a sputtering fuse. The fuse was attached to a keg of gunpowder.

There was a brilliant flash of light, then a loud blast as the planted bomb exploded. The back wall of the jail came crashing down into the alley, and a moment later, a short, bandy-legged man, coughing and waving at the cordite-strong smoke, picked his way through the rubble.

"Are you all right, Ray?" Win shouted.

"Yeah!" Ray answered, still waving at the smoke and the powdered brick hanging in the air as a result of the pulverized wall. The dust from the explosion had peppered his beard, making it look white.

Win and Joe rode up to him, leading the third horse. Ray swung into the saddle. Then the three horses bolted into a gallop as if they were shot from a cannon. So complete was the surprise that no one even saw them leave.

7

WIN, JOE, AND RAY WERE AT THE SALCEDO WAY STATION, a gray, weather-beaten building which sat baking in the afternoon sun. A faded sign just outside the door of the building gave the arrival and departure schedule of stage-coaches that no longer ran, for a line that no longer existed. The stage line had been abandoned three years earlier when the railroad reached Brownwood from Lampassas.

The roof and one wall of the nearby barn were caved in, but there was an overhang at the other end that provided some much-needed shade for their horses. Ray was sitting on the front porch with his back against the wall. Win was inside the building, looking around at what remained of a once-busy passenger station.

Joe was outside, by the pump. A little earlier, he had taken the pump apart, and now he was reassembling it.

Win stepped back out onto the front porch.

"Find anything interesting in there, Win?" Joe asked from his position, bent over the pump.

"Not really," Win answered. He looked down at Ray. "All right, Ray, we've done our part. We came to San Saba like you wanted. We even busted you out of jail. Now it's time for you to tell us what this is all about.''

"I've told you all I know," Ray replied.

"Tell us again."

"I met a fella some weeks back in a saloon back in Henderson. He said his name was Al Summers. We got to talkin' some 'bout what we done durin' the war, and turns out our paths musta crossed, only we just never know'd it. I mean, me an' him had never run acrost each other before, but he know'd lots of the same folks we know'd. Like ole' Bill Anderson, and George Todd. Hell, he even know'd Quantrill.''

"They're all dead," Win said.

"I know they are dead. What's that got to do with anything?''

"It means we have no way we have of checking him out.''

"He's all right," Ray said.

"How do you know?"

"I can feel it."

"That's it? You feel it?"

"Win," Joe said, looking up from the pump. "We went by Ray's feelin's a lot durin' the war, and he never steered us wrong.''

"Yeah," Ray said. "Why you doubtin' me now?"

Win paused for a minute, then nodded. "Joe's right," he said. "All right, Ray, if you think this Al Summers is tellin' you straight, then that's good enough for me. Now, tell us the rest again.''

"After he found out I once rode with Quantrill, he asked me could I round up any of the other fellas who was still around. Right off, that put me to wonderin'. I mean they's paper out on nearly all of us, so I was thinkin' what if this guy's a bounty hunter? Wouldn't that be an easy way to catch some of us? So I asked him what for.

" 'I've got a little job in mind,' he says.

" 'What kind of job?' I asks.

" 'One that'll let you and the fellas you round up make a lot of money,' he says.

" 'I'm always lookin' for some easy money,' I says.

" 'This ain't exactly takin' candy off a babe. You goin' to have to take some risks,' he says.

" 'What kind of risks?' I asks.

" 'Same kind of risks you took when you was ridin' with Quantrill,' he says. 'Only this time, you'll get to keep a lot more of what you take.' "

"But he didn't say how much?" Win asked.

Ray shook his head. "He just said there was a lot of it. More'n any of us had ever seen before."

"What do you think, Win?" Joe asked.

"I think if there is a lot of money, we'd better be getting an equal share," Win replied. "If we share equally in the risk, then we are going to share equally in the money."

"He didn't say nothin' 'bout whether the share would be equal or not. He just said there'd be lots of money," Ray said.

"Equal," Win said again.

"What if he won't go along with that?" Ray asked. "I mean, it's his plan. He may figure he deserves more. And I don't want to pass up the deal, not if it means a lot of money."

Win smiled. "My reckonin' is that he'll go along with it. He really has no choice. He can't do it alone, or he wouldn't have asked us in on the job. And it's too late for him to get anyone else."

"Hey," Joe called, smiling broadly as he began working the pump handle up and down. "Hey, you fellas, look at this! It's moving real smooth now! I think I fixed it."

"Don't do no good to have a working pump if there ain't no water down there," Ray said.

"There's water down there," Joe answered. He started toward the barn.

"Where you goin'?" Ray asked.

"To the horses. I'm going to get my canteen so I can prime the pump."

"Joe, wait a minute! Do you think that's a good idea?" Win asked. "If you use up all your water trying to prime this pump, there's no telling where we're going to find some more."

"There's water down there, Win. I can smell it. Only we ain't going to get it if the pump ain't primed."

"You use all your water up, don't think you're goin' to get any of mine," Ray warned him.

"Hell, as I recall, it ain't your water anyway," Joe called back. "I seem to mind that you was in jail. We had to dig up a horse and tack for you."

Joe returned a moment later with his canteen. He unscrewed the cap and held it over the pump for a second, then, with a shrug of resignation, poured it in. The water glistened brightly in the sun, then gurgled as it all rushed down the pipe.

Joe began working the handle. "It's comin'!" he said. "I can feel it!"

Win moved over to the pump, and even Ray stood up to watch.

Suddenly the suction was broken, and the pump handle began to move easily again.

"Damn!" Joe said. "I lost it."

"Tole' you," Ray said, moving back over to resume his position on the porch.

"Win, let me have your water."

"Joe . . ."

"Come on, Win, it was almost there. I could feel it. Think about it. Wouldn't some cool deep-well water taste good about now? And there would also be plenty of water for the horses. And a bath! Win, hell, we could even take us a bath!"

"A bath?" Ray said. "Why the hell would you want to take a bath? Out here, you'll just get dirty again."

"You sure there's water down there, Joe?" Win asked.

"I'm tellin' you, Win, it was right there. I just lost the suction, that's all."

"All right," Win finally agreed. "I'll get my canteen."

Ray sat back down on the edge of the porch, reached down to pull up a straw, then stuck the end of it in his mouth. "You two boys is crazy, you know that?" he asked. "You're throwin' away good drinkin' water on the chance there might be some in that well. And for what reason? So's you can take a bath."

Win came back a moment later, carrying a canteen. He handed it to Joe, who then poured it into the top of the pump. Once again, Joe began pumping.

"Yes!" he said, after a moment. "Yes, it's coming!"

Win stood by watching with intense interest, and again Ray came over to see what was happening.

"Shit!" Joe shouted. "Shit, I need some more water to hold the suction. It's almost there, but I may lose it. I need more water!"

"Well, don't look at me," Ray said. "You ain't gettin' my water."

"We already got your water," Win replied. "That was your canteen I just got."

"What?"

Win started toward the horses again. "Don't lose the suction, Joe. I'll get my canteen."

"Hurry!" Joe called.

Win ran to his horse, got his canteen, then ran back.

"Pour it in while I'm still pumpin'," Joe said.

"You crazy sonsofbitches!" Ray shouted. "You've used up ever' damn bit of our water!"

Ignoring him, Win began to pour as Joe continued to pump.

There were more gurgling sounds as the water disappeared down the pipe. For several long, anxious seconds, Win and Ray watched as Joe continued to pump, the only sound being the squeak and clank of the pump handle and piston.

Suddenly a big smile spread across Joe's face. "Get ready," he said. "Here it comes!"

At that moment, water began pouring out of the mouth of the pump. For the first few seconds, the water was red with rust. Then it cleared.

"Look at that!" Joe said. "Ain't it beautiful the way it's flashin' and sparkling like that? Why, it looks like I'm pumpin' pure sunlight!"

Win cupped his hands under the cascading water, then bent down to take a drink.

"How is it?" Ray asked anxiously. "How does it taste?"

Win took several, deep swallows, then stood up with water running down his chin.

"Oh, that's fine!" he said. "Joe, you remember when we were with Quantrill and we hit Shawnee Station?"

"Yes."

"We got some champagne there, remember?"

Joe smiled. "Yeah, I remember. We got two cases of it."

Win pointed to the water that was still cascading down from the pump. By now the water splashing on the ground was beginning to form little rivulets.

"Well, Little Brother, that champagne wasn't half as good-tasting as this."

"Yahoo!" Joe said. "Here, you pump! Let me have a drink!"

Win took over the pump while first Joe and then Ray drank their fill. Next they filled their canteens. Then they found a bucket and took water to the watering trough for their horses.

Finally, they dragged another trough over to the pump so they could pump water directly into it. When it was full, they stepped back to look at what they had done. Ten thousand points of light danced on the undulating surface.

"There you go, Big Brother. It's ready for your bath."

"No," Win said. "It was your idea, and you are the one who fixed the pump. You go first."

Joe smiled broadly, then began stripping out of his clothes.

JOE HAD FINISHED HIS BATH, AND WIN, WITH HIS CIGAR titled at a jaunty angle, was sitting in the tub toward the end of his own bath, when the three riders arrived.

"Here they come," Ray said, shielding his eyes. "The fella on the right is Al. Don't know the other two."

Joe came around to stand with Ray as they waited for the riders. Win didn't get out of the water.

"Wasn't sure you would be here," Al said to Ray. "Word I got was that you got yourself throwed in jail and was goin' to get hung."

"I was in jail," Ray replied. He smiled. "But my two pards here busted me out."

"These the boys you was talkin' about? The Coulters?" Al dismounted and walked over to the water trough, then splashed some water on his face.

"This is them. The one takin' the bath is Win. The big ugly one is Joe."

Al was lanky and rawboned, with a handlebar mustache. One of the two riders with him was a big man, almost as large as Joe, though perhaps twenty years older, with salt-and-pepper hair and beard. The third rider was small and clean-shaven. This rider seemed to be eyeing Win with a bemused expression.

"You goin' to introduce them two?" Joe asked,

Drying his face with his bandanna, Al nodded toward the riders who had come in with him, neither of whom had yet dismounted.

"The big fella there is Jeb Finley. He was a colonel with General Jo Shelby."

"Colonel Finley, I've heard of you, sir," Win said.

"And I have heard of you, Mister Coulter," Finley replied.

"And this is—" Al said, but he was interrupted by Win standing up in the water. As the water only came to a little above his knees, his nudity was completely exposed.

"Mister, I see you've been eyein' the bathwater," Win said easily. "I'm finished now, you're welcome to it if you'd like a bath."

"Jessica Moore," Al finished.

Jessica took off her hat and shook her head, allowing long tresses of fire-red hair to cascade down around her shoulders.

Seeing that it was a woman, Win sat down again, so quickly that he splashed water everywhere. Jessica laughed.

"Goddamnn, Al, you could'a said somethin' sooner," Win said.

"Why, Mr. Coulter," Jessica said in a soft, husky voice. "It doesn't say much for me that you can't tell I'm a woman just by looking."

"Well, you had your hat pulled so low, and those pants and that shirt," Win sputtered.

Jessica laughed again. "You don't have to explain," she said. "I dressed this way purposely. Until this is all over with, I'm going to have to pass as a man."

"Yes, well, you *ain't* a man," Win said. He held out his hand and moved it in a small circle. "So if you would, please, just turn around until I get out of here and get dressed."

"Really, Mr. Coulter. I've already seen you. What is there to hide now?" Jessica continued to appraise him with her cool, green eyes. Her lips were curled in the suggestion of a smile, which accented her high cheekbones.

As Win studied her, he began to wonder how he could have mistaken her for a man. He could see now that she was really quite a pretty woman.

"I reckon you're right at that," he said, standing up again.

Jessica had actually been teasing him, and had no idea he would call her bluff. When he stood up to expose himself again, she was caught off guard, and she cleared her throat in embarrassment.

"Perhaps I *should* give you a little privacy," she said, turning her horse around.

"By the way, Miss Moore," Win said as he began drying off. "My offer still goes. If you want to take a bath, you're welcome to take off your clothes and jump in the water."

"Thank you, Mr. Coulter," Jessica replied. "You will understand, I'm sure, if I decline your generous proposition."

"If you folks will climb down, I'll take your horses," Ray offered. "There's water and shade for 'em over to the barn."

"Thank you," Finley said as he dismounted. By now, Win had pulled on his trousers, and Finley looked back toward Jessica. "You can turn around now, my dear," he said. "Mr. Coulter is decent."

"Thank you," Jessica said. She too dismounted, and handed the reins of her horse to Ray.

Win began to rewrap the bandage around his waist.

"Oh, you are wounded!" Jessica said.

"Yeah, I had a run-in with a couple of Mexicans."

"It looks very recent," Jessica said. "When did it happen?"

"About four days ago," Win answered.

"Mr. Summers," Finley said. "I told you to get responsible men, not men who are likely to get into bar fights."

"You said get someone like Quantrill's Raiders," Al replied. "Well these, here fellas ain't *like* Quantrill's Raiders. They *are* Quantrill's Raiders. And that means they ain't Sunday School teachers."

"It wasn't a bar fight, Colonel Finley," Joe explained. "And my brother didn't start it. But if you don't want us in on this, just let us know and we'll be going on our way."

"No, no," Finley said, holding up his hand. "I'm sorry if I seemed judgmental. It's just that in order for this to work, we are going to have to have as much self-discipline as we do skill and daring."

"We can be as disciplined as we need to be," Win said. "For our fair share," he added. He dropped one end of the bandage, and had to start reapplying it.

"Here, you'd better let me help," Jessica suggested, stepping over to take the bandage wrapping from him.

"Thanks."

Jessica started wrapping the bandage around him, carefully and skillfully. When her fingers touched his skin, they managed to be hot and cool at the same time.

"You do this well," Win said.

"I have a knack for it," Jessica said.

"Colonel, you want to tell us what this is all about?" Win asked, looking up at Finley.

"All right," Finley answered. "But first, I think I need to tell you a little about General Jo Shelby. You men knew him, of course?"

"Commanding general of the Missouri Cavalry," Joe said. "Of course we knew him."

"What you may not know is that, after the surrender, General Shelby decided to keep his men together. We left Missouri and marched through Arkansas and Texas, all the way to the Rio Grande, where, rather than surrender our flag, we buried it in the river."

"I heard you all had done something like that," Win said. Jessica was finished with the bandaging, and he began putting on his shirt.

"Something happened during that last mission that has a bearing on what we are about," Finley continued. "As we passed through Austin we learned that a group of brigands and deserters had taken it upon themselves to loot the state treasury. And although it wasn't our state, it wasn't our money, and it wasn't even our cause, General Shelby decided that our honor lay in dispersing the robbers and saving the money for the people of Texas."

"You did that?" Joe asked.

"We did that, yes. We killed nearly all of the robbers and returned the money."

"You had your hands on all that money and you returned it?" Ray asked. He shook his head. "General Shelby must've had a great deal of control over his men to convince them to do that."

"If you remember General Shelby, you know that is so," Finley said. "But I must tell you, if we had known then what we know now, I don't believe even General Shelby would have returned that money to the vault."

"Why do you say that?"

"Less than one week after we passed through Austin, the Union Army arrived to begin their occupation duty. The first thing they did was take the money from the vault and transfer it to the Federal Treasury."

"Hell, what did you expect, Colonel? The Yankees won," Win said.

"I could accept that if all the money they took had made it to the Federal Treasury," Finley said. "But less than one half of the money reached the Federal Government. The commanding general of the Tenth Kansas Cavalry Brigade siphoned off the rest of it. He then resigned from the army, and has subsequently used that money to bribe tax collectors and buy himself a sheriff. He now owns much of this land and most of the businesses in the towns. He's turned San Saba County into his own little kingdom."

"You must be talking about Jason Bellefontaine," Win said.

"Yes," Finley said. "You've met him?"

Win shook his head. "I haven't met him, but I have heard all about him. And I met some of his hirelings."

"Ah, you would be talking about his sheriff, Angus Buford," Finley said. "Perhaps you ran across him before? He was a first sergeant in Emil Slaughter's company of Jayhawkers. Slaughter's Jayhawkers, of course, being a part of Bellefontaine's Tenth Kansas Cavalry Brigade."

"Emil Slaughter?" Win asked sharply.

"Yes," Finley said, stroking his salt-and-pepper beard. "The same Emil Slaughter you killed when Quantrill hit Lawrence."

"Colonel, if ever there was a man needed killin', it was Emil Slaughter," Joe said.

"Believe me, I'm not finding fault with his being killed," Finley said. "I know the story of what happened at your family farm, how Slaughter murdered your father, raped and murdered your mother, then burned all the buildings."

"Let's change the subject," Joe suggested.

"Of course," Finley said. "I can see how that might not be something you would care to remember."

"There's another fella I met in San Saba," Win said. "An ornery young cuss named Tim Tyrell. Do either of you know anything about him?"

"I know quite a bit about him, Mr. Coulter," Jessica said. "He is my brother."

"Your brother?"

"My half-brother, to be more accurate," Jessica said. "We had the same mother, but different fathers. When Tim's father died, my mother married my father. Tim's father was from Kansas, my father was from Texas. When the war began, my father returned to Texas and my mother and I came with him. Tim stayed in Kansas with an aunt and uncle on his father's side."

"I'm sure you must've asked yourself why we would have a woman involved with this job," Finley said, then. "Perhaps it will help you to understand when I tell you that the uncle Tim Tyrell stayed with is General Jason Bellefontaine."

"What does that have to do with Miss Moore?" Win asked. "She just explained that Jason Bellefontaine is Tyrell's uncle, not hers."

Jessica dipped her handkerchief into the water and wrung it out.

"Jason Bellefontaine may be my brother's uncle," she said as she began patting her face with the wet cloth.

She aimed a penetrating stare at Win.

"But he is my lover."

8

IT WAS DARK.

Win was sitting on the edge of the porch, eating peaches from a can. The meadow between the building and the tree line glowed in a soft luminescent yellow from the winking of hundreds of fireflies. High overhead, the black-velvet sky was filled with stars which ranged in magnitude from pulsating white all the way down to a barely perceptible blue dust.

Win had taken his supper with the others inside the building, then come outside to eat his peaches and get a breath of fresh air. Colonel Finley had not yet filled them in on what he had in mind, though he'd promised to do that before everyone bedded down for the night.

Win heard someone walking across the porch behind him. Without turning around, he spoke.

"Evenin', Miss Moore."

"That's very good," Jessica said. "How did you know it was me?"

"Your steps are lighter and quicker than the others," Win said. He held out his can. "Would you like the rest of my peaches?"

"Why, how nice of you to share," Jessica replied, sitting on the porch beside him.

"I have sort of a weakness for canned peaches," Win admitted. "I almost always have three or four cans in my saddlebags." He chuckled. "I'm not sure my horse appreciates my habit."

Jessica pulled a spoon from her shirt pocket and began eating.

"They are very good," she said as she took the first bite.

"Miss Moore, may I ask you a question?"

"It's Win, isn't it? Win, don't you think you could call me Jessica now? I mean, we are going to be working together."

"All right, Jessica, but that is my question. If your brother is Bellefontaine's nephew, and if you are his woman . . ."

"I am *not* his woman," Jessica said quickly, interrupting Win in mid-sentence.

"I thought you said . . ."

"I said he was my lover," she told him. "There is a difference. I have no more feeling for him than a whore does for the men who visit her."

"Then why?"

"I do it for the same reason the whores do it," Jessica said. "Only, I will be getting a lot more money than any whore has ever gotten."

"Then it is just the money?"

"Yes," she answered quickly. Then, after a pause, she said, "No. It's not just the money."

"What else?"

"I told you that when the war started my father moved us to Texas. When he got here, he joined the Confederate army. During the war he led a patrol into Kansas. He was caught, and even though he was in uniform when he was caught, he wasn't treated as a prisoner of war. Instead he was tried as a spy, and he was hanged.''

"I'm sorry to hear that," Win said.

"General Bellefontaine could have interceded on my father's behalf. My mother wrote to him, begging that he do so, but she got no answer from him. After the war, when he came to Texas, he told my mother and me that he never received the letter, and that he didn't know about my father until it was too late.

"We believed him. Then his wife died and he offered me a job managing his household. It seemed like a respectable enough position, with good pay, so I accepted.

"But one day, when I was looking for something, I happened to find in his papers my mother's letter to him. I also found a letter from General Halleck suggesting leniency for my father. Most damning of all was General Bellefontaine's answer to General Halleck. 'As the Federal Government has not recognized the Confederacy as a legitimate government, then it follows that their army is not a legitimate army,' he said in his letter. 'Therefore I believe the sentence of death I have imposed upon Major Moore to be correct.' '' She sighed. "I think it was the fact that he lied to us that disturbed me more than anything else. He swore to us that he did not know about my father until it was too late, when in fact, he was the one who ordered my father's execution."

They were silent for another moment. Then Jessica continued. "That was when I decided I would kill him."

"I reckon I can understand you wantin' to kill him, all right," Win said. "But sleepin' with him seems to me to be a funny way of doin' it."

"Perhaps not," Jessica replied with a wry smile. "Do you know why the black widow spider is called a black widow?"

"No, I can't say as I do."

"It is because after she mates with the male spider, she kills him."

"Damn," Win said. "I'm glad I'm not a male spider." He looked at her and smiled. "Although I guess if I got randy enough, I might be willin' to take the chance. Especially if it was with someone who looked like you."

Jessica smiled at his comment, then continued with her explanation. "I figured letting Bellefontaine into my bed would allow me to gain his confidence, which would make things easier. I started out thinking I wanted to kill him, but when I found out just how much money he has managed to steal since coming to Texas, I came up with another idea. Losing all of his money would be worse than death to him. And it would be much more profitable for me."

"And that's about the time Colonel Finley got in touch with you?"

"Not quite," Jessica said. "Colonel Finley didn't recruit me. I recruited him."

"You mean . . . this is all *your* idea?"

"Every bit of it," Jessica replied.

At that moment, Finley stuck his head through the door.

"Jessica, my dear, Mr. Coulter, would you two like to come inside? I think it's time we went over the plans."

Win stood up and brushed off the seat of his pants. "Yes, indeed, I am ready," he said. "I don't want to miss this." He held out his hand to help Jessica to her feet.

INSIDE, ON WHAT HAD BEEN THE TICKET COUNTER, FINLEY spread out a large hand-drawn map. He kept the corners from rolling back up by the application of four disparate weights: a rock, a pistol, a can of beans, and a coffeepot.

"Gather round the map now," Finley said.

The map showed a stretch of railroad, with all the adjacent terrain features clearly marked.

"Next Wednesday a two-car train will make a run from San Saba to Lampassas," Finley said. "One car will be General Bellefontaine's private car. The other will be an express car. Gentlemen, this is no ordinary express car." Finley pointed to the lower right-hand side of the paper, to the drawing of a railroad car.

"The walls of this car are reinforced with steel, so that they are bullet-proof. It is also fitted front and rear on both sides with firing slots. But what makes it most dangerous is this." Finley tapped the end of his pencil on something that stuck up from the top.

"What is that? A smokestack?" Al asked.

"That is a turret," Finley explained.

"A turret?" Joe asked. "What is a turret?"

"It is a cylinder with a gun attached, fitted so it can turn three hundred and sixty degrees. It's not an original idea. I'm afraid the designer of this car borrowed the concept from Mr. Ericson's ironclad ship, the *Monitor*. This ability to turn means that one man, protected by the steel sides of the turret, can spin all the way around to face a threat, no matter from which direction it may be posed."

"I'll be damned," Ray said.

"And there is something else," Finley added. Again, he touched the turret with the end of his pencil. "The gun that will be firing through the firing slit on this turret is probably unlike any gun any of you have ever seen before. It is capable of extremely rapid fire."

"That would be a Gatling gun?" Win asked.

Finley looked up in surprise. "Yes. Are you familiar with the Gatling gun?"

"I've never seen one, but I have heard of them," Win

said. "They're guns with several barrels and you turn a crank to make them all fire fast."

"Yes. That crank not only rotates the barrels, it also ejects the old cartridges and loads new ones," Finley said.

"Lordy, wouldn't I love to see that, though?" Joe said.

"I'm afraid you will see it, Mr. Coulter," Finley said. "Unfortunately, you will see it from the wrong side."

"Colonel, you've made your point as to how difficult it is going to be to stop this train," Win said. "Now, tell us why we *should* stop it."

"Why, to get at the money the express car is carrying, of course."

"That's my next question. How much money is in there?"

Finley smiled. "I know that some of you have been wondering just what Miss Moore's role is in all this. I'm going to let her answer the question as to just how much money we are talking about."

"The amount of money the express car will be carrying that day is three hundred thousand dollars," Jessica said.

"Whew!" Ray said, whistling.

"That's fifty thousand dollars each," Win said quickly.

"Not quite," Finley said. "Not all shares will be equal."

"Colonel, you just described a train car that is built like the *Monitor*, and you expect us to go up against it. We'll do it, and we'll get the money it's carrying. But we're going to divide it equally."

"I'm afraid you don't understand," Finley began, but Jessica cut him off with a raised hand.

"There are some others involved," Jessica said. "Their cut is one hundred thousand."

"Will the others be taking the same risks?" Win asked.

"No," Jessica said. "But they are necessary."

Al and Joe looked at Win. He ran his hand through his hair, then nodded.

"All right," Win finally said. "I reckon I can go along with that."

"Good," Jessica said, obviously relieved that there wouldn't be a problem. "Colonel, you want to go on with your plan?"

"Very well," Finley said. He pointed to the express car again. "As long as this Gatling gun is operating, one man can hold off an entire troop of cavalry. So, the first thing we have to do is get rid of the turret."

"Any ideas?" Ray asked.

Finley shook his head. "All I've come up with so far is *what* has to be done. Just *how* it is to be done is yet to be worked out," he answered.

"All right, what else has to be done?" Win asked.

"The train has to be stopped. The guards in the express car have to be taken care of. The doors to the car have to be breached, and once we are inside, the vault has to be opened."

"It's easy enough to stop the train," Joe said. "All we have to do is pull up some of the track."

"That won't work," Jessica said.

"Why not?"

"Bellefontaine is no fool. He knows that this train is going to make an attractive target, so he is sending a pilot engine and a track repair crew half an hour ahead," she explained.

"And even if we got it stopped, there is still the problem of the express car and the Gatling gun," Finley said.

"What if we buried a bomb under the track?" Win suggested. "We could set it off just as the train arrives."

"That could get some innocent people killed," Jessica said.

"Who on board that train is innocent?"

"The engineer and fireman," Jessica suggested. "They are both men with families just trying to earn a living. And then, of course, there is me." She smiled. "Although I'd be the first to admit that calling me innocent begs the term."

"Wait a minute. *You're* going to be on that train?"

"She has to be," Finley said.

"Why is that?"

"Because once you do get the train stopped and get into the express car, I am the only one who can open the vault for you." She smiled. "I know the combination."

"There you have it, gentlemen, all the details," Colonel Finley said. "Surely, if we all put our heads together, we will come up with a workable plan."

9

ALTHOUGH EVERYONE HAD THROWN THEIR BEDROLLS down inside, Win woke in the middle of the night feeling hot and stuffy. Thinking it would be cooler outside, he got up a little after midnight, gathered his bedroll, then picked his way quietly through the snoring, sleeping bodies.

He spread his blankets out on a small, grassy knoll about fifteen yards from the building and lay down. The stars were so clear and bright that he almost felt as if he could reach up and pluck one from the night sky. He saw a falling star, and he spent a moment wondering what caused them to sometimes become dislodged.

A creaking sound on the front porch caused him to grab his pistol and raise up quickly. He looked toward the source of the sound, then saw that someone else was abandoning the building. At first, whoever it was was hidden in the shadows of the porch. Then the person walked over to the pump and into a silver splash of moonlight.

It was Jessica.

Win almost called out to her. Then he took in a quick, sharp breath as he saw her start taking off her clothes.

Win remained still and quiet as Jessica removed her shirt,

then stepped out of her pants. She had been wearing a camisole under her shirt, and that came off too. She was wearing nothing under the pants.

Jessica walked over to the trough, which still held the water that both Joe and Win had used for their bath. She lifted a long shapely leg over the edge of the trough, tested the water with her toe, then stepped down into it. She sat down, but even then her breasts were still exposed, the curving globes silvered by the moonlight, the nipples dark but clearly visible. Win watched her at her bath, feeling himself grow erect at this unexpected and enticing view.

Finally Jessica finished and stood, like Aphrodite emerging from her bath, and stepped over the edge of the trough. Then, still wet and naked, she started walking toward Win.

Win was surprised—first that she knew he was there, and second that she was displaying no sense of embarrassment or anger at having discovered him. She sat down beside him with as little concern about her nudity as if she were fully dressed and this had been a chance encounter on a busy sidewalk in the middle of the day.

"I'm sorry about watchin' you take your bath," Win said. "I didn't mean to be spying on you. But I was already out here and I didn't realize what was happening until it was too late. I didn't want to embarrass you."

Jessica turned her face toward him and studied him for a long moment with a rather whimsical smile on her face.

"Did you enjoy the show?" she asked in a throaty voice.

"Well, yes," Win admitted, surprised by the question. "I must confess that I did."

"Good. Then we are even," she said.

"Even?"

"I had my own show this afternoon, remember?"

"Yes. I remember."

"I saw you get up and take your bedroll outside," Jessica said.

"You mean, you *knew* I was out here when you came to take your bath?"

"I knew," Jessica said.

From the barn a horse whickered, and Win saw Jessica shiver as the night breeze passed across her drying, naked body. He examined the tightly drawn nipples on her uplifted breasts, the long supple lines of her legs, and the shaded invitation at the junction of her thighs.

"Are you cold?" he asked.

"A little," she said.

Win lifted his blanket and held it out toward her. She moved toward him. Then he wrapped it around her, drawing her nude body against his.

"Better?"

"Much."

They were silent for a moment.

"Win, what is it like?" she asked.

Win was confused by her question. "What is what like?"

"To live the life of an outlaw? To be as free as a bird, to go where you want, when you want, and to be beholden to nobody?"

"That sounds good to you, does it?"

"Yes."

"I didn't plan this life, Jessica." Win pulled up a stem of grass, then began sucking on the cool, sweet root.

"What kind of life did you plan?"

"I figured I'd be a farmer, marry some girl from a neighboring farm, or maybe from town. By all rights I should be raising a couple of kids about now, worrying about rain and helping my neighbors put up a barn or a granary."

Jessica laughed softly. "It's hard to imagine you as a farmer, Win Coulter."

Win laughed with her. "Yeah," he said. "Well, to tell you the truth, my pa shared your opinion. 'You was born to hang,' he used to say."

"I guess the war changed the plans of a lot of people," Jessica said.

"I reckon so."

"What are you going to do with your money?"

"Nothing."

"Nothing?"

"I've got this funny habit," Win said.

"What's that?"

"I don't spend money until I actually have it in my hands."

"Don't you even like to think about it?"

"No."

"Well, I know what I'm going to do," she said. "I'm going to San Fran—" She stopped. "Come to think of it, maybe it would be better if I were more like you. There's no sense in my spending money I don't have."

"Money doesn't mean anything anyway," Win said.

"How can you say that?"

"If you've got enough money for a good horse and saddle, enough to keep a few necessary items in your saddlebags . . ."

"Like canned peaches?" Jessica interrupted.

"Like canned peaches," Win agreed. "Plus a few coins to buy yourself a steak dinner, have a few drinks, play some cards, and get someone to warm your bed for a night or two . . . what need is there for more money?"

"Well, I'm not going to cook a steak dinner for you, Win Coulter," Jessica said. He felt her hand then, moving across his thigh, stopping to rest over the mound caused in the front of his pants by the erection he had from sitting next to such a beautiful naked woman. "But I'll warm your bed if you'd like."

"I'd like," Win said. He undid his belt, unbuttoned his pants, then slid them down across his legs, taking them and the boots off at the same time. It being summertime, he was wearing no underwear. He took off his shirt, and within a moment was sitting beside Jessica as naked as she was.

Jessica's hand traced a path across Win's skin. Then she wrapped her fingers around his erection, feeling its incredible heat and throbbing power.

"Oohh," she breathed. "I had no idea."

"What?"

"This . . . this *thing*," she said, squeezing his penis. "I've only been with Bellefontaine. I thought all men would be pretty much the same." She began moving her hand up and down his cock, making a tactile exploration of it.

When Win felt her long cool fingers closing around his erection, a web of flame shot through his body.

His fingers went to her thighs, slipped through the hair, and spread the moist lips. She was incredibly wet, hot, and moaning with desire.

"Oh . . . oh, my!" she said. "So this is what it can be like!"

Win kissed her, thrusting his tongue into her mouth. She opened her eyes in surprise, then, with an eager little squeal, pushed his tongue out of her mouth with her own and began probing his.

Win laid her back onto the blanket, then moved over her. Jessica raised her legs and spread her knees for him, then put her hand on his penis again and guided it inside her.

"Oh . . . oh, my!" she said again as he pushed himself deep inside her.

Win began thrusting, and she raised her hips to meet him,

taking him down inside her, sliding him across every nerve ending within. She gasped with the pleasure of it, and cried with the joy of it as she built toward fulfillment. To Win, it was as if her senses were like a restless willow in a windstorm, moving, tightening, latent with the promise of more.

Win felt her when she climaxed. Unable to hold back her cries of joy, she let moans of pleasure escape her lips, and threw her arms around Win and pulled him to her. Win felt himself coming and he pumped harder, deeper, and faster.

Afterward, they fell asleep in each other's arms. Much later, Win was awakened by an extremely pleasurable sensation. When he was fully awake he became aware of two things. Jessica was sucking his penis, and she was lying on top of him, grinding herself into his face. He had only to put out his tongue and it slipped through the musky fur and into the wet slit that was above him.

Once she knew that he was awake and was fully participating in her game, she began thrashing and moaning, sucking and licking, nibbling and squeezing, until Win came again, feeling it blast out of him, wondering how she could hang on during such an eruptive orgasm. Then he knew by the throbbing, pulsating muscles in the thighs she had locked to either side of his face that her orgasm was every bit as explosive as his own.

Sometime before morning, she got up from his bedroll and padded, still naked, across the grass over to the porch, where she got dressed, then went back inside. He put his own clothes back on, then went to sleep.

"DAMN, BIG BROTHER, YOU PLANNING ON SLEEPING YOUR life away?" Joe asked.

Win opened his eyes and saw Joe squatting on his

haunches, looking over at him. Joe was holding two steaming cups of coffee, and he handed one cup to Win.

"Thanks," Win said, sitting up. He looked around and saw that several of the others were up. But he didn't see Finley or Jessica.

"Finley and Miss Moore still asleep?" he asked.

"Asleep? Hell, no," Joe answered. "They got up and left before the sun come up."

"I'll be damned," Win said. What he didn't say was how he admired someone who could screw all night and still have the strength and energy to get up and leave before sunup.

"Come on inside," Joe invited. "You've got some plannin' to do."

"*I've* got some planning to do?" Win asked as he pulled on his boots. "What do you mean *I've* got some planning to do?"

"How we're going to get the train stopped and get into the express car," Joe answered. "I told the others you were really good at figuring out stuff like that."

"Oh, you did, did you?"

"Yep," Joe said, smiling broadly. "So they decided to put you in charge."

"Put me in charge? I thought Colonel Finley was in charge."

"Ah, you know how colonels are," Joe said. "They're big ones for tellin' you what do to, then sittin' back an' lettin' you do it. When it comes time to hit the train, it'll be just us. And I'd feel a heap better about you leadin' us than I would if it was Al or Ray."

10

JASON BELLEFONTAINE WAS A VERY LARGE MAN. THE MEN who worked for him were fond of saying that he would "dress out" at over 350 pounds. Rather than try to hide his weight, he played it up, wearing ruffled shirts and a gold watch chain which stretched across his vest. He didn't wear a beard, but had bushy muttonchop sideburns framing jowls which hung like saddlebags from each side of his face. He had no visible neck. Instead, a series of chins started somewhere just under his rubbery lips, then trailed down to the top of his chest.

Bellefontaine was sitting at a large, polished mahogany table in his dining room, and he reached for a little silver bell, then picked it up and shook it. The melodic dinging brought a young, attractive Mexican woman out of the kitchen.

"*Sí*, Señor General?" she asked.

"Maria, I would like you to bring me some more pancakes," Bellefontaine said.

"*Sí*, Señor General."

"Oh, and Maria?" Bellefontaine called as she started toward the kitchen. Maria stopped. "Only about ten or twelve this time," he said. "I'm just about full."

"*Sí,* Señor General."

When Maria left, Bellefontaine looked toward the opposite end of the table. This morning he had ordered Maria to set a place for Jessica, but she had not yet returned. He was a little irritated by her absence. She had told him she was going to visit her mother and that she would only be gone for four days. He had expected her yesterday.

He heard the front door open and close, and when he looked up, he saw Tim coming into the dining room.

"Uncle Jason, we've got the Gatling gun mounted in the turret now, and we're ready to test it."

"Tim, how many times have I told you not to call me Uncle?"

"I know. You said it's because of the men," Tim said. "But I thought when we were alone . . ."

"It's not just because of the men. It's for you as well. If the men hear you calling me Uncle, then they will not give you the respect you deserve. They will be convinced that you attained your position by way of family connections, rather than through your own initiative."

"Yes, sir," Tim said.

"The fact that it's true, that you hold your position only because of a promise I made to my late wife, makes no difference. The men must think you are one of them."

"Yes, General."

"And another thing," Bellefontaine continued. "There had better never be another example of what happened last week. It is being said all over the county that you hired a couple of Mexicans to take care of a personal problem for you and because of that, one of them is blind in one eye and the other has a cracked rib."

"If they were unable to handle the job, they shouldn't have taken it," Tim replied.

"Maybe not. But the fact remains you hired someone else to fight your battles. It doesn't look good, not for you, and not for me. See that it doesn't happen again."

"Señor General, your pancakes," Maria said, returning with a plate piled high with the steaming cakes.

"Thank you, Maria," Bellefontaine said. He scooped three tablespoons of butter from the butter tub. Then, as the butter melted and cascaded down on every side, he poured on a generous amount of syrup. "Has your sister returned?" he asked Tim.

"No, sir."

"I want you to go to your mother's house and get Jessica. She was supposed to be back last night."

"I'm sure she'll be along soon," Tim said.

Bellefontaine took a large bite of pancakes, then spoke with his mouth full.

"I intend to see that that is so," he said. "Because you are going to fetch her back here."

"Yes, sir," Tim said, obviously not pleased with the task. At that moment, however, he happened to look through the dining room window and saw Jessica arriving, driving a buckboard. "What did I tell you?" he said. "There she is now."

"Good. Will you tell her I would like to see her, please?"

"Yes, sir. What about the test of the Gatling gun?"

"You see to it."

Tim smiled broadly. "Yes, sir!" he said. "I'll be glad to!"

A MOMENT LATER JESSICA CAME INTO THE ROOM. SHE WAS wearing a long blue dress and a white straw hat, having changed from the men's clothes she had worn when she was at Salcedo. She smiled brightly.

"Did you miss me while I was gone?" she asked, coming over to kiss Bellefontaine on his cheek.

"I thought you were going to be back yesterday," he said petulantly. "You said four days."

"I'm sorry. Mother wasn't feeling well, so I stayed a bit longer than I intended."

"No harm done," Bellefontaine said, reaching up to take her hand in his. "As long as you're back."

Jessica looked at his soft, fat hand on hers, and she compared it to Win's broad, strong hand. Then she thought of Win's hand on her body, and she shivered.

"You must have some of these pancakes," Bellefontaine said, totally missing the shiver. "They are quite good this morning."

THREE STRAW-DUMMY TARGETS WERE SET UP APPROXI-mately one hundred yards away from the turret-mounted Gatling gun on top of the express car. Tim climbed up into the seat behind the Gatling gun, placed the one-hundred-cartridge magazine into position, sighted on the targets, then began turning the crank.

The gun roared loudly, filling the inside of the turret with eye-burning gunsmoke and red-hot shell casings. He saw dust kicking up all around the straw dummies, and from the dummies themselves. The head of one of the dummies was completely cut off by the stream of bullets.

Tim began yelling in excitement as he twisted the crank, and he continued to do so until the last bullet was expended and there was only the rattle and click of the rotating empty barrels.

When the gun was empty, Tim hopped down, then ran out to examine the targets.

"Son of a bitch!" one of the other men said as he too went over to look at the straw dummies. "I've never seen such a thing. Hell, if we'd'a had these guns durin' the war, we would'a whipped you Yankee sonsofbitches bigger'n all hell."

Tim looked at him. "Yes, but you didn't have them," he said. "We did."

"Reckon you're right," the unreconstructed Rebel said. "Figured there had to be some reason the damn Yankees won."

BELLEFONTAINE HELD A CELEBRATION DOWN AT THE DE-pot. The volunteer fire department was there, and so was the municipal band. Free food and beer were being served to all who showed up. The occasion was the official chris-tening of the Bellefontaine Express Car.

Bellefontaine made a short speech, thanking everyone for coming.

"As many of you know, I have bought the bank since I came to this fair community," Bellefontaine said. "And I have invited you here today to see the great care I will give to the money that is entrusted to me. Not only while it is in the bank itself, but also whenever it becomes necessary to ship species from one location to the other. Behold, the Bellefontaine Express Car!"

Bellefontaine held his hand out toward the car. As if on signal, the covers over the two firing slits dropped down, and rifle barrels were poked through. At the same time the turret on top, which had been facing away from the crowd, spun around so that the wicked barrels of the Gatling gun were facing the crowd. Those who were close enough could see Tim's face just inside the turret.

The crowd gasped, and several women emitted little screams.

Bellefontaine laughed. "Don't worry, ladies and gentle-men," he said. "This is only a demonstration, designed to show you what any potential train robber would see if he were foolish enough to attempt to stop this train.''

Tim began turning the crank and the Gatling gun started rattling in rapid fire, the bullets slamming into a large target pinned to the side of a wagon load of hay.

The women screamed in alarm, and the men shouted in surprise, as large chunks of the target were ripped away by the stream of bullets.

As abruptly as it started, the gunfire stopped, and for a long moment there was nothing but the haunting sound of returning echoes.

Finally the shocked crowd regained their voices, and dozens began shouting as one.

''Hey, General, you goin' to let us inside that thing to have a look around?'' one of the voices called from the crowd.

''I'm afraid that wouldn't be prudent,'' Bellefontaine said. ''I'm certain that any potential robber would love to know what the inside of this car looks like. But I don't intend to share that information with them.

''I will tell you this, however. The express car is equipped with the latest model of vault. It is called an American Standard. The door is four-inch-thick steel, and it is locked by four steel bars, each two inches in diameter. In addition, the tumblers are absolutely silent so that no one can pick the lock.''

''What if someone blasted it open?'' someone in the crowd called.

''Ladies and gentlemen, you could literally fill this train car with gunpowder, then set it off. The car would be turned into kindling wood, but the safe would be unscratched,'' Bellefontaine said proudly.

"It sounds pretty secure, all right," one of the towns-people said.

"Yes," Bellefontaine replied. He looked over toward the constable. "Would that our jail were as secure."

11

THE BUCKBOARD CREAKED AND GROANED AS BELLEFON-taine stepped out of it and onto the wooden platform that surrounded the depot in San Saba. There were nearly one hundred people gathered around to watch the departure of Bellefontaine's special train.

The engine, which was painted dark green with yellow filigree, rode upon huge red driver wheels. It was trimmed out in highly polished brass, and it glistened brightly in the morning sun.

The express car was also green, with Bellefontaine's name rendered down the side, in yellow script. The express car was followed by Bellefontaine's special car, also green, a luxurious vehicle complete with a bedroom, dining room, and kitchen facilities. That was followed by a red caboose. In addition to the train crew and guards, a telegrapher would be making the trip. The telegrapher, who would ride in the caboose, had an instrument, complete with wire clamps, which would allow him to tap into any telegraph line to send a message.

There were a total of six guards, including in the number Sheriff Buford and Tim Tyrell. Tim would be riding in the turret.

When the buckboard arrived, Angus Buford stepped out of the express car and walked over to greet Bellefontaine.

"General, the steam is up and everything is ready," he said.

"Is the money aboard?"

"Yes, sir, it is," Buford replied.

Bellefontaine looked around. "Where is Miss Moore?" he asked. "She should be here. She came into town earlier this morning."

"She's on the train, General," Buford said. He nodded toward the second car. "In your private car."

The dispatcher and the train conductor came out of the depot then. The conductor was carrying a sheaf of papers.

"Is everything arranged?" Buford called to the conductor.

"Yes, sir," the conductor replied, holding up the papers he was carrying. "We have track clearance all the way to Kansas City."

"Then, gentlemen, I suggest we get under way," Bellefontaine said. Puffing from the effort, he walked across the platform, then climbed up into his car. He smiled when the aroma hit him.

"I wasn't sure if you'd had time for breakfast this morning," Jessica said, greeting him at the door. "So I fried some ham and baked some biscuits."

"You did it yourself?"

"Yes. I know you have servants running all over the house, but I wanted to show you that I could be quite domestic, given the opportunity."

"Well, that's very nice of you, Jessica," Bellefontaine replied. "Actually, I did have breakfast before I left, but I wouldn't be adverse to a small snack."

"Good. I would hate to think I went to all this trouble for nothing. Now, how do you want your eggs?"

"Fried, over easy, I suppose. But only about half a dozen."

"You have a seat at the dining table, General. I'll have your eggs ready for you by the time the train leaves the station."

OUTSIDE, THE CROWD WATCHED AS THE ENGINEER OPENED the throttle. There was a hiss, followed by a sudden puff of steam. Metal creaked and groaned. Then the piston began to slide out of the cylinder, pushing the connecting rod against the driving wheels. The engine started forward, taking up the slack at the drawbars between the cars until, with a clacking jerk, the entire train was in motion.

The engineer blew his whistle, and a team of horses, sitting at the crossing just beyond the depot, reared. The train, consisting of a powerful engine and a short string of cars, was able to gather speed quickly, and by the time it was at the end of town, it was moving much faster than anyone had ever seen a train travel.

Christina watched the train until it was out of town, then went into the depot and wrote out a telegram.

> TO BILL JONES STOP SORRY TO HEAR ABOUT
> JOHN'S CONDITION STOP FIRST MEDICINE LEFT
> HALF HOUR AGO STOP AM SENDING SECOND SHIP-
> MENT NOW STOP

She tore out the page and handed it to the telegrapher. "Send this to Dallas, please."

"A relative?" the telegrapher asked.

"I beg your pardon?"

"The fellow who is ill. John. Is he a relative?"

"Oh. Yes, he is my cousin."

"Would you care to include a love, Mrs. Rawlings? It would only cost six more cents."

"No, what I have written is fine, thank you."

"Very well. That will be seventy-two cents," the telegrapher said.

Christina gave him the money. Then he sat down at the table and began to send the signal.

"That's funny," he said after he operated the key.

"What?"

"The key isn't as crisp as it should be."

"What does that mean? Is the message getting through?"

"Oh, yes, you don't have to worry about that," the telegrapher said. "It's a little slower, that's all, like more than one receiver is connected." He smiled. "Sometimes they do that in the bigger towns, like Dallas. They'll have an instrument down at the depot, and another one in a separate telegraph office."

THIRTY MILES EAST OF SAN SABA, FIVE HORSES WERE grazing peacefully in a grassy meadow near the track. Al was pacing nervously up and down the track, while Win, Joe, and Colonel Finley were sitting on a small grassy knoll alongside the track. Actually, only Win and Finley were sitting. Joe was lying down, with his hands folded behind his head.

Ray was sitting cross-legged beneath a telegraph pole, holding a sending and receiving instrument in his lap. Already this morning he had intercepted half a dozen telegrams, but he had discounted them all as being not important.

Suddenly the machine started clacking. Al looked up from where he was on the track. Win, who was sucking on the root of a grass stem, tossed it away. Joe sat up. Colonel Finley walked over to stand beside Ray.

Ray nodded. "This is it, boys. This is what we've been waiting for," he said. He began writing. After the clacking stopped, he read the message:

> TO BILL JONES STOP SORRY TO HEAR ABOUT JOHN'S CONDITION STOP FIRST MEDICINE LEFT HALF HOUR AGO STOP AM SENDING SECOND SHIPMENT NOW STOP

"We've only got half an hour between the pilot engine and the train," Win said. "That doesn't give us much time."

"Where are we going? To the bridge?" Joe asked.

Win nodded. "The bridge," he said.

CHRISTINA'S FATHER AND UNCLE CHARLEY GIBSON WERE in the jailhouse, drinking coffee. Although repair had started on the back wall of the jail, it was not yet completed, and therefore there were no prisoners in custody. The few drunk and disorderly cowboys Constable Gibson had rousted during the last week had been released, either on their own recognizance or to the custody of their employer. For anyone with a more serious charge, provision had been made to transport him to the jail over in Lampasas.

"Did you send the message?" Matt asked his daughter as she came in the front door.

"Yes," Christina said, pouring herself a cup of coffee.

"I hope everything goes all right," Matt said.

"If I know the Coulter brothers, we have nothing to worry about. They are the best when it comes to things like this," Gibson said.

"Yes, but are you absolutely positive these are the Coulters?" Matt asked. "They claim their name is Carver."

"Well, they would hardly use their real name," Gibson

said. "Especially when they saw that their friend was about to hang. But they are the Coulters, all right. I saw them during the war, when Quantrill spent a winter here in Texas. I recognized them right off . . . but I didn't say anything because I didn't want to scare them away."

"Then that brings up the next question," Matt said. "And it's a big one."

"I know what you are going to ask. Can we trust them?" Gibson said.

"Well, can we?"

Gibson rubbed his chin. "I don't know. Right now they don't know anything about our involvement. When they find out . . . well . . . we'll just have to wait and see how they take it."

"And if they don't take it well?" Matt asked.

"I asked that same question to Colonel Finley and he said let him worry about it, so that's just what I'm going to do. And I suggest you do the same."

"Well, I'm not worried about them at all," Christina said. I've never met anyone like Win before. I would be willing to put my fate entirely in his hands."

"I'm glad you feel that way, my dear, for that is exactly what you have done," Gibson said.

As Christina recalled her time with Win, she felt an involuntary shiver of pleasure pass over her, and she looked up quickly to see if her father or her uncle had noticed her reaction. When she saw that they had not, she smiled, then sank back into the warmth of her memory.

WIN, JOE, AND AL WERE HIDING IN SOME BUSHES, JUST out of sight from the track. They had a large bucket of grease with them. Ray had left a few minutes earlier, but now he came running back. Only Finley was missing. He had taken the horses ten miles down the track. If everything went as planned, the men would get on the train, take the money, and then be off at about the place where Finley would be waiting. That way they would have fresh horses ready for their getaway.

"The pilot engine is just now coming around the curve," Ray said, panting from the exertion of his run.

"Okay, boys," Win said. "Get ready. As soon as the pilot engine has passed, we have less than thirty minutes to get the rails greased and get up on the trestle."

"How much grease do we have to put down?" Al asked.

"I'd say at least one hundred yards," Win said. "Otherwise the train won't lose traction long enough to amount to anything."

"Thirty minutes isn't much time to put down one hundred yards," Joe said.

"Yeah," Win agreed. "And we may not even have that much time if the train has caught up any with the pilot engine."

The pilot engine came by then, the engineer leaning out of the right cab window, staring ahead down the track. The engineer had a prominent chin, a hooked nose, and a very thin mouth so that nose and chin gave the illusion of nearly touching. The engine hurried by with a hiss of steam and the whirring sound of steel rolling upon steel. It pounded out onto the trestle, thundering in its reverberations. Then, as quickly as it had arrived, it was gone.

"All right!" Win shouted. "Let's get that grease down!"

The four men climbed up to the track and began applying a thick layer of grease onto the rails. As they put it down, the grease glistened blackly in the noonday sun.

After only a few minutes, they heard a whistle in the distance.

"Damn, it hasn't been anywhere close to thirty minutes!" Joe said in agitation.

"Yeah, I was afraid they might have closed the gap between them," Win said. He grabbed the bail of the bucket, then slung the remaining grease far out into the bushes. "All right, boys. Up onto the trestle," he ordered.

"Win, how much do you reckon we got done?" Joe asked.

Win looked at the track. "I would say no more than fifty yards," he suggested.

"You think fifty yards of grease is going to be enough to do the trick?"

"It has to be. Remember, we don't have to actually stop the train. All we have to do is slow it enough to allow us to drop down onto it from the top of the trestle."

"I'm not all that happy about dropping down onto a moving train," Al said.

"You'll make it all right," Win said. "All you have to think of is what will happen to you if you don't. If you miss it, you'll be stuck out here without your horse and without your share of the money."

Al grinned sheepishly. "I reckon that's enough proddin', all right."

"Son of a bitch!" Joe said, grinning broadly. "We're goin' to do it, ain't we? By God, we're really goin' to pull this off."

"If we all do our part," Win agreed.

They climbed on top of the trestle.

"Now all of you, lay down!" Win ordered. "We can't take any chances on the engineer or fireman seeing us!"

Once again the approaching train whistled and this time, when the boys looked up, they could see it coming around the wide, sweeping curve the track made on its approach.

"Get ready!" Win shouted.

The sound changed when the train hit the long grease slick. There was a sudden acceleration of the steam-relief valve. The great driver wheels lost traction, then began spinning. The train jerked and clacked at the sudden change in its propulsion dynamics, then slowed considerably.

"WHAT'S HAPPENING TO THE TRAIN?" BELLEFONTAINE asked the conductor. "Why are we slowing down?"

"That happens on occasion, General," the conductor replied, looking out the window. "If a section of rail gets flattened out a little, it sometimes gets very slick and the wheels lose traction. I expect we'll be across it in a moment."

Looking out the window as well, Jessica saw that they were passing onto the trestle. Then she saw something else, something that she didn't want the conductor to see.

"Conductor, would you ask the porter to bring some more coffee, please?"

"Yes, ma'am," the conductor said, turning away from the window.

"And another one of those cakes," Bellefontaine called toward the conductor as he started up the aisle.

Jessica continued to look out the window at the shadow the train cast onto the water, and on the opposite bank of the Lampassas River. The shadow showed four men dropping, one by one from the trestle, onto the top of the train.

12

AS SOON AS THEY HIT THE TOP OF THE TRAIN THEY HAD to lie on their stomachs to make certain they weren't knocked off by the cross-beam at the far end of the trestle. Win found a supporting rod running the length of the top of the car, and held onto it as he watched the support timbers flash by. By now the train had moved through the greased part of the track, and was beginning to build up speed again as it threw off the grease that had built up on the driver wheels.

Once they were clear of the trestle, Win lifted his head up to look ahead. Almost immediately his eyes began to water from the smoke that was rolling back from the engine. He turned his face away, blinked a few times, coughed, then looked around to make certain everyone else had made it.

They all had, and they were now lying on top of the car, holding on against the wind and the jerking movement of the train.

Win got their attention, then pointed toward the opening of the turret. He made a waving motion with his hand to indicate that they should move to the side of the car, just above the door, while at the same time warning them to stay away from the turret opening so that they couldn't be seen.

"Joe, have you got the smoke pot?" he shouted above the wind and the roar of the train.

"Yes, I've got it," Joe answered, patting the haversack he was carrying. He pointed toward the turret. "Looks like we got lucky, Win! There's no one on watch!"

"Yeah," Win replied. "They are either very confident or very stupid." Win looked toward Al and Ray, and saw that they had moved into position, ready for the next step.

The plan was to introduce the smoke pot into the express car by dropping it down the turret. For now, the car was tightly closed, but when the smoke started pouring out, Win knew those inside would be forced to open the big side door. As soon as the door slid open, the raiders would swing down from the top of the car and let themselves in. They would have the benefit of surprise, plus the advantage of fresh air, whereas those inside would be partially blinded and perhaps confused by the smoke.

"All right, Joe, let's do it!" Win said.

Using his body as a shield against the wind that was being generated by the train's velocity of forty-five miles per hour, Joe struck a match, then lit the fuse on the smoke bomb. He held the bomb until the first bit of smoke began to stream out, then dropped it down through the opening in the turret.

Almost immediately, smoke started gushing out of the turret opening.

"Get ready!" Win said to the others. "That door's going to slide open any minute!"

The men waited, lying on the edge of the car, looking over the edge toward the still-closed side door. From the turret behind them, smoke continued to boil.

The door didn't open.

Win and the others looked at each other in confusion.

"What the hell?" Joe asked. "Ain't they breathin' in there?"

"You sure you got that smoke bomb all the way inside?" Al asked.

"It went all the way," Joe insisted. "I heard it hit the bottom."

"Well, somethin's wrong," Ray insisted. "How could they stay in there with all that smoke?"

By now the bomb was nearly spent, and the smoke coming from the turret was beginning to grow thinner.

"I'm going to look down inside," Win said.

"Win, be careful!" Joe called. Win nodded, then still on his belly, wriggled back up to the top of the car. He got into position behind the turret, then raised his head and peered over the edge, looking down inside.

The inside of the car was so dark and smoke-filled that, at first, he couldn't see anything. Then, when he could see, he saw nothing, not anyone, and not any movement. He raised up from the turret with a puzzled expression on his face.

"What is it, Win? What do you see?" Joe called to him.

Win shook his head.

"That's just it," he said. "I don't see a damned thing. You'd think there would be someone moving around down there."

The train whistle blew.

"What do we do, Win?" Joe asked. "We've got to get inside. We're going to be up to where the horses are pretty soon."

Win looked around for a second, then nodded as if just making up his mind.

"We're going to stop the damned train," he said.

"How?"

"The old-fashioned way. By sticking a gun in the engineer's face."

Standing up, Win, Joe, and then Al and Ray started running forward on top of the express car. They jumped from the car down onto the tender, then moved through the piles of wood until they reached the back of the engine.

At that precise moment, the fireman turned to pick up some more wood. When he saw Win and the others, his eyes grew wide with fright. Win cocked his pistol and pointed it at him, and the fireman backed up with his hands in the air.

"What the hell's got into you?" the engineer asked when he observed the fireman's strange behavior. He turned around then, and seeing Win and the others, raised his hands as well.

"Stop the train," Win ordered.

The engineer shook his head. "Can't do that," he said. "I got orders from General Bellefontaine not to stop for any reason."

"Is General Bellefontaine standing here holding a gun on you?" Win asked.

"No, sir," the engineer said, shaking his head.

"Well, by God, I am," Win growled. "Now, stop the goddamned train, or I'll shoot you where you stand and stop the train myself."

"All right, all right!" the engineer answered urgently. He pulled on the brake handle, and the wheels locked, bathing the inside of the engine cab with a shower of sparks thrown up from the action of steel wheels sliding on steel rails.

The train decelerated so rapidly that Win had to grab something to keep from falling. The fireman, seeing that as his opportunity, picked up a poker and started toward Win.

He got no more than a few steps before Joe dropped him with a solidly thrown punch.

Finally, with squeaks, rattles, hisses, and pops, the train came to a complete stop. The engineer moved the relief valve to vent off the excess steam, and the engine hissed and snorted like some living creature.

"What did you do to my fireman?" he asked.

"He'll be all right when he comes around," Joe insisted. "Pulling a damn fool stunt like that, he's lucky he wasn't killed."

"Get down from the engine," Win ordered. He nodded toward the prostrate fireman. "And take him with you."

"What . . . what are you going to do?"

"Nothing," Win said. "I just want to make certain you don't do anything either. I wouldn't want this train pulling off without us."

Groggily, the fireman started to get up, and the engineer helped him to his feet. Then the two men, under the direction of Win, jumped down to the ground.

Win, Joe, Al, and Ray got off as well, then started walking toward the rear, keeping close to the cars in order to minimize their exposure to anyone who was on the train and who might take a notion to fight.

From the back end of the private car, a black man climbed down and began looking around.

"You the porter?" Win asked, suddenly stepping out from between the cars.

The black man had not seen Win, and his eyes grew wide in shock when Win spoke. He nodded.

"Yes, sir," he said.

"Who else is in the car with you?"

"General Bellefontaine, he be in the car. So do Mr. Kelly, the conductor. And Miss Moore, she be in there too."

"Anyone else? Any guards?"

The porter shook his head.

"No, sir."

"Anyone in there armed?"

Again, the porter shook his head. "No, sir. All thems with guns is in the 'spress car with the money," he said.

Win stepped up behind the porter. "Let's go into the car," he said.

Walking behind the porter, Win climbed the steps into the car. The entry passageway was narrowed by the bathroom and kitchen. After a run of fifteen feet, the passageway opened up into the lounge area, and there Win saw Bellefontaine, now out of his seat, looking through the window, trying to figure out what was going on.

" 'Scuse me, General Bellefontaine," the porter said.

"What is it? What did you find out?" Bellefontaine asked gruffly. "Why did that fool engineer stop?"

"Perhaps this here gentleman can tell you," the porter suggested.

"What gentleman?" Bellefontaine asked. He turned then, made curious by the porter's statement. Win pushed the porter to one side and pointed his gun at Bellefontaine.

"Good morning, General Bellefontaine," Win said.

"What are you doing on my train? What do you want?"

"Why, I've come to rob it, of course," Win answered easily. "But I'm going to need your help."

"Help? You're asking me to help you steal?"

"It should be easy enough for you, General, since you stole all the money in the first place," Win said. "Besides, if you don't order your guards to open the door to the express car, I'm going to shoot you."

"You're bluffing."

"I'm afraid he isn't bluffing, General," Jessica said, smiling at Win. "Don't you recognize him?"

"Recognize him? No, I don't. Should I?"

"I would think so," Jessica said. "Especially as he and his brother, and the men they rode with, caused you a considerable amount of difficulty during the war. Besides, their faces have decorated half the posters in Texas for the last few years."

Bellefontaine's eyes narrowed. "My God, I do recognize you," he asked. "You're the Coulter brothers, aren't you?"

"I'M WIN," WIN SAID EASILY. "MY BROTHER, JOE, IS outside."

Bellefontaine put his hand inside his jacket, and Win cocked his pistol, the metallic click making an ominous sound. "General, your hand had better come back out of there slow and empty," he said.

"I . . . I was just getting a handkerchief," Bellefontaine said nervously. His hand shaking, he held the handkerchief out to validate his claim.

Win nodded, and Bellefontaine began to wipe the sweat from his face.

"What about it, General?" he said. "Do you help us? Or do you die?"

"I'll . . . I'll help you," Bellefontaine said.

Win made a waving motion with his gun. "Let's go," he said.

Win ordered everyone off the car so he could keep an eye on them. Then they walked forward toward the express car where Joe, Ray, and Al were still standing close in, out of the line of fire of anyone who might suddenly appear at the gun ports.

"You!" Bellefontaine said, pointing to Al. "You are in league with men such as these?"

Win was surprised by the apparent recognition, and he

looked at Al suspiciously. "You two know each other?" he asked.

Bellefontaine, sensing an advantage, smiled. "Mr. Coulter, allow me to introduce someone from the other side. This is Al Santos. You have no doubt run into him before. He is the man who killed Bloody Bill Anderson."

"You was a Jayhawker?" Ray asked.

Al nodded contritely, then looked at Win. "Win, I'm sorry about not bein' straight with you boys," he said. "Wasn't sure you'd want anything to do with me if you knew who I really was."

"No wonder the only ones you said you know'd was dead," Ray said. "Hell, you kilt 'em."

"Of them three that I named, Captain Anderson is the only one I killed," Al said. "Though I fought ag'in you boys enough, I reckon I killed my share of your friends . . . and I reckon you killed your share of mine."

"And now, you are in league with bushwhackers," Bellefontaine said derisively. "You are a traitor, sir."

"No, sir, I ain't no traitor, General," Al said. "During the war, I was true blue to the Union. But the war is over now, and we're all goin' our own paths. You got your way of gettin' rich . . . I got mine. And if they was one thing I learned durin' the war, it was that the bushwhackers did what they did better'n anyone I ever saw. Seemed to me like if I was goin' to put my trainin' to use, it might as well be with the best. So, here I am."

"Santos, did you ever ride with Emil Slaughter?" Joe asked coldly.

Win held up his hand. "No, Al, don't answer that!" he said quickly.

"Win," Joe said, but Win shook his head.

"Let it go, Joe," he said.

"What do you mean, let it go? Slaughter's the one that raided our farm, killed Ma and Pa."

"Slaughter's dead and the war is over," Win said.

"For us, the war ain't ever over," Joe insisted.

"I reckon it's not over for Al either," Win said. "But the way I look at it, the enemy has changed. And now men like Al and us are on the same side."

Al nodded. "I'm glad you feel that way," he said. He looked at Joe. "And Joe, I will answer your question. I wasn't with Slaughter, but I have to confess that I done things just as bad as anything Slaughter ever done."

Joe was silent for a long moment. Then he shrugged. "Hell," he finally said. "So have I. And I reckon Win's right. We're on the same side now."

"Good move, General, trying to get us to fight among ourselves," Win said. "But it didn't work. Now get this door open."

"Hell, we don't need him for that," Ray said. "Why don't we just kill the sonofabitch and blast the door open?"

"No, no!" Bellefontaine said. "Buford! Buford, open the door! They've got me covered! Open the door, they'll shoot if you don't!"

Bellefontaine's shout was met with silence.

"Win, there's somethin' fishy about this," Joe said. "We ain't heard a sound since we stopped the train."

Win raised his pistol and pointed it at Bellefontaine. "Try again," he ordered.

"Buford, I'm ordering you to open the door!" Bellefontaine said. He stepped up to the door and banged on it. When he did, it slipped open about half an inch, and he jumped back in quick surprise.

"Win!" Joe said. "The door ain't locked!"

"Yes, I see," Win answered.

Pistols at the ready, the men stood by, waiting for the door to be thrown open.

Nothing happened.

"Get ready," Win whispered.

Stepping up to the door he suddenly shoved it open. A few dying wisps of smoke drifted out, but nothing else.

Win stepped up to the open door and looked inside. "Ray, give me a boost up," he said.

Ray made a stirrup with his hands, and Win climbed up into the car. Although most of the smoke had dissipated, enough of it remained to hang in the bars of sunlight that splashed in through the open door. Win saw someone lying face-down on the floor, and he knelt beside him, then rolled him over. There was a bullet hole in his forehead. He dragged him over to the door.

"Who's that?" Joe asked.

"It's Dobbs, my accountant," Bellefontaine said. "You didn't have to kill him."

"We didn't kill him," Win answered.

"What do you mean, you didn't kill him? If you didn't, who did?"

"Maybe the same one who did that," Win said, pointing across the car toward a vault. The door of the vault was wide open, and the shelves inside the vault were bare.

"My money! What happened to my money? Buford!" Bellefontaine leaned his head into the car and looked around. "Buford, where are you?"

"If you want my guess, find the money and you'll find Buford."

"That thieving, double-crossing bastard!" Bellefontaine swore. "The guards are gone too, aren't they? They were all in it together. Buford, the guards, my worthless nephew. All in it together."

Win looked around the car, then glanced up. He saw something that held his gaze for a moment.

"No," he said. "I don't think Tyrell was part of the deal." He pointed to the top of the car.

"What is it?" Jessica asked anxiously. She stepped up to the opening of the car, then looked up toward the turret. Tim, who was obviously dead, was slumped forward against the unused Gatling gun. "Oh," she said. "Tim. Poor Tim."

13

ONE HOUR BEFORE WIN AND THE OTHERS DROPPED DOWN from the overhead trestle onto the top of the express car, the train had stopped for water. When it did so, Buford stepped over to the door and pushed it open.

"Sheriff, you shouldn't be opening the door like that," Dobbs said.

Buford looked around at the accountant. The small man, who was wearing a green visor, was sitting on a three-legged stool near the vault.

"Why the hell not?" Buford growled.

"General Bellefontaine left strict orders this door is not to be opened until he says so."

"Is that a fact?"

"Dobbs is right, Buford," Tim called down from his perch up in the turret.

"I'm just having a look around," Buford explained.

"You don't need to. I can see everything from up here," Tim said. He put his hands on the ring that surrounded the turret and began turning it through the full 360 degrees. "There's no one out there except the fireman, and he's putting water into the tank."

"What about you, Shaw? You see anything?" Buford asked.

Rufus Shaw, one of the four guards, looked out through the firing slit in front of him. "I don't see a thing," he answered.

Peterson, McCloud, and Lomax, the other three guards, also reported that all was clear.

From outside the train, they could hear the fireman and engineer calling back and forth to each other.

"Get ready, boys, we're about to get under way again," Tim said. "The fireman just put the water spout back up and has climbed into the cab."

"Good, good," Buford said. He looked at the four guards and nodded, and they returned his nod.

"Dobbs," Buford said. "Open the safe."

"I beg your pardon?" Dobbs replied.

"I said open the safe."

"I . . . I don't know if I should do that," Dobbs said. "General Bellefontaine was very clear in his directions."

Buford pulled his pistol and pointed it at Dobbs. "I'm glad to see that you follow instructions. Now, you let me be clear," he said. "Open the goddamn safe or I'll blow your brains all over the inside of this car."

"Sheriff Buford, what are you doing? Are you robbing the general?"

"Yes," Buford said. "I'm robbing the general."

Dobbs looked around in fear, desperate for one of the guards to come to his aid. The expressions in their faces told him, however, that not only not going to come to his aid, they were themselves part of the robbery.

Shaw stepped up close to him. "Are you going to open the safe, Dobbs?" he asked. "Or do you need persuading."

"Get out of the way, Dobbs!" Tim suddenly shouted. There was a gunshot from above, and Shaw went down.

Peterson returned fire, and Tim grunted in pain, then slumped forward, his gun falling to the floor.

"Damn!" Shaw said in a strained voice. "I didn't know that sonofabitch had a handgun up there with him. I thought he just had that Gatling."

Buford stepped up to Dobbs.

"I'm . . . I'm not going to open the safe for you, Sheriff," Dobbs said.

"You don't have to, you little bastard," Buford growled. "I know the combination." He put the gun to Dobb's forehead and pulled the trigger.

Less than a minute later he had the safe open. The money inside was in five large cloth bags, and he started passing it out, one bag to each person. When he held a bag out toward Shaw, he stopped and pulled it back.

"Give it to me," Shaw said.

"You think you can keep up with it?"

"Yes," Shaw said. "I'm not hurt that bad."

Buford paused for a moment, then handed the bag to Shaw. "You lose it and I'll kill you," he said.

"I'm not going to lose it."

With all the moneybags passed around, Buford took out his watch and looked at it.

"All right," he said. "We should be to where the horses are. Everybody out, now!"

Buford slid the door open. Shaw came to the edge, paused for a moment, then jumped out. After Shaw the others went out, one after the other, until it was Buford's turn. With one hand, Buford grabbed hold of the firing slit, then moved outside to hang along the side of the car. With the other hand he pulled the door closed so that, when the train went around curves, no one would notice that the door was open. When the door was pulled shut, he pushed himself away from the car, hit on the down-slope side of the track bed, rolled several times, then got up and brushed himself off.

Buford had purposely left the car last because, by his calculations, it put him nearest the horses. It was his way of discouraging any of the others from deciding to strike out on their own with the money they were carrying. The effectiveness of his plan was proved when he found the horses right where he expected them to be. He then had a leisurely wait of some fifteen minutes before the others showed up. None seemed the worse for their leap from the train, though Shaw was obviously suffering from his gunshot wound.

THE LITTLE GROUP OF FIVE RIDERS PUSHED HARD ACROSS the purple sage. Buford figured that they had put at least ten miles between themselves and the railroad track. And since the train had continued on even after they jumped from the car, that meant that by now the train had to be at least another forty miles away. He smiled at the way things were going. By the time the robbery was discovered in Dallas, they would be so far away that no one would ever catch up to them.

This robbery was the culmination of a year of work on a plan to divest Bellefontaine of his money. Buford had come up with one idea after another, discarding each idea as being unworkable almost as quickly as it had been conceived. His break had come when Bellefontaine told him that he was beginning to be nervous about keeping so much cash on hand. When Buford suggested that he deposit his money in the local bank, Bellefontaine laughed.

"In San Saba? Have you taken a good look at that bank? It has a safe that could be opened by a child, or blown open with a firecracker! I may as well keep my money hidden in a mattress. No, sir. My money is going to Kansas City where they have a real bank.''

"Kansas City? How are you going to get it there?'' Buford asked.

"By train.''

"Train?''

"A very special train,'' Bellefontaine said.

Bellefontaine then asked Buford if he would take personal charge of recruiting a guard detail that would oversee the transfer of his money to the bank in Kansas City. Smiling broadly because he could see that the way to Bellefontaine's money had finally been opened to him, Buford agreed immediately.

Buford had let neither the clerk, Dobbs, nor Bellefontaine's nephew, Tyrell, in on the plan. As he thought back on it now, he realized he should have paid more attention to Tyrell, but who would have thought the cowardly little bastard would have the guts to put up a fight. It would've gone off without a hitch if Tyrell hadn't shot Shaw.

Thinking of Shaw, Buford turned in his saddle to see how Shaw was doing. Shaw was slumped forward in his saddle, one hand holding onto the pommel, the other stretched across his stomach. The hand he held across his belly was red with the blood that had spilled through his fingers. Peterson was riding alongside solicitously, leading Shaw's horse.

"Buford,'' Peterson said. "Buford, we got to stop for a while and give Rufus a rest.''

"Shaw took his chances, just like the rest of us,'' Buford replied.

"Hell, look at him, Buford! He can't hardly even sit up no more, let alone ride.''

"Buford, we could all use a little rest,'' Lomax said.

"Yeah,'' McCloud added. "Hell, what with the train still

goin' and all, we must be near fifty miles away by now.''

"All right, there's a stream just ahead, under that clump of trees," Buford said. "We'll stop there, give our horses a blow, and fill our canteens.''

"Thanks," Peterson said. "Did you hear that, Shaw? We're goin' to stop and rest for a bit.''

Shaw nodded weakly.

It took the riders another couple of minutes to reach the clump of trees. Buford held up his hand and they stopped, then dismounted.

"This is a good place to stop," Lomax said. "We've got shade and water.''

"McCloud, get up on that hill and take a look around," Buford ordered. "Make sure there's no one following us.''

"Who the hell would be followin' us?" McCloud replied.

"Just do what I say," Buford ordered.

"Lomax, help me get Rufus down," Peterson said.

Buford watched as the two men gently pulled Shaw from his horse, then laid him down. Shaw stretched out on the ground with his eyes closed and his breath coming in ragged, shallow gasps.

"How is he?" Buford asked.

"He's hurt real bad, Buford," Peterson said. He pulled Shaw's hand away, and Buford saw that his entire stomach was covered with blood. "He needs a doctor or he's goin' to die.''

"And just where do you plan to find a doctor?''

"I don't know. Maybe Lampassas.''

"So we go riding into Lampassas about the same time they discover the train has been robbed and two men killed and they send a telegraph message back," Buford said. He shook his head. "You're not being very smart.''

McCloud came back down the hill then. "Ain't nobody for miles around," he said.

"Didn't think there would be. But it didn't hurt to check," Buford said.

"What about him?" McCloud asked, nodding toward Shaw.

"What about him?"

"What are we goin' to do about him?"

"Nothing," Buford said succinctly.

"Nothing? We can't just let him lie here and do nothing," Peterson complained.

"Why the hell not?"

"Because he's one of us. It could be me, or Lomax, or McCloud, or even you lying here."

"That's right," Buford agreed. "And if it was one of us, we'd be in the same boat."

"What if I go into town to get a doctor and bring him out here?" Peterson asked. "I could be back before tomorrow mornin'."

"Tomorrow morning? Look at him, for God's sake," Buford said. "He's been gutshot. You ever know anyone to live after bein' gutshot? Doctor or no doctor, he'll be dead before tomorrow morning."

"Still, it don't seem right not to do somethin' about it."

Buford smiled. "I'll tell you what I'll do. Whenever he croaks, I'll let the rest of you divide up his share."

"You know, Buford, now that you bring it up, that's somethin' else I been wantin' to talk about," Lomax said.

"What's that?"

"The shares," Lomax said. "The way you're dividin' things up."

"What's wrong with the way I'm dividing things up?"

"It ain't right, is all," Lomax said. "I mean, you givin'

us only fifteen hunnert dollars apiece, while you're takin' all the rest yourself.''

"Now you're gettin' an extra five hundred dollars each," Buford said. "And that was the deal I gave you when you agreed to come with me."

"Maybe so, but it ain't right," Lomax said. "We took the same risk you did. Hell, look at Shaw. He got himself shot. The way I look at it, we deserve a lot more'n any fifteen hunnert, or even two thousand dollars. By my thinkin', it ought to be share, an' share alike.''

"Is that right?" Buford asked. His voice was thin and cold.

"Yeah, that's right. And the way I look at it, there are three of us. I figure if need be, we can make you see things our way.''

Without the slightest change of expression, Buford drew and shot, his bullet raising dust from Lomax's shirt as it penetrated just below the sternum.

"My God!" McCloud shouted in sudden alarm.

Lomax's face reflected more shock than fear, for Buford's sudden action had caught Lomax completely by surprise. He let out a loud whoosh, as if the air had been driven from his body. Then his eyes rolled up into his head and he fell backward, landing heavily. He flopped once, then was still.

Peterson and McCloud looked on with a sense of shocked disbelief. Buford turned toward them with the smoking pistol still in his hand. The expression on his face had not changed in the least, and seeing him like that, so totally impassive even though he had just killed a man, was somehow more frightening than if his face had reflected rage.

"You boys just got another seven hundred and fifty dollars each,'' Buford said. ''Unless you want to argue about it?''

''No, no!'' McCloud said, shaking his head and holding his hands out in front of him, as if warding Buford off. ''I'm perfectly happy with how you're doin' things.''

''I am too,'' Peterson said.

''I'm glad we understand each other,'' Buford said. He put his gun away. ''Throw the money sacks on Lomax and Shaw's horses,'' he said. ''We'll make pack animals out of them.''

''What about them?'' Peterson asked.

''What about who?''

''Shaw and Lomax.''

''Leave 'em.''

''Buford, you can't just leave them here like this,'' Peterson said. ''I mean . . .''

''You want to stay with them?'' Buford asked.

''No!'' Peterson answered quickly. ''It's just like I told you, I hate to leave Rufus here without tryin' to do somethin' for him. After all, me 'n him's been pards for a long time, now.''

McCloud walked over to look down at Shaw. ''Yeah, well, you and him ain't partners no more, Peterson,'' he said. ''Shaw's dead.''

14

RAY KINGSLEY WAS BEGINNING TO WONDER IF HE HADN'T made a mistake when he left the Coulters. They did offer to let him stay with them for a while, and they were good men who he was proud to call friends. Jesse and Frank James were good men too, and so were the Youngers. So were all the men he had ridden with during the war.

There were some who talked about the war, and how bad it was, but not Ray Kingsley. If he could have it his way, the war would still be going on. During the war he had never been hungry, never without a drink, and most importantly, never without friends. Things were quite different now, when he was broke some of the time, hungry most of the time, and lonely all of the time.

Ray was beholden to the Coulters for busting him out of jail, particularly as he was about to be hanged. But he didn't want to stay with them. They were brothers and sometimes, even though they didn't mean it, he actually felt more alone when he was with them than he did when he was by himself.

Right now, Ray Kingsley was sitting in the Silver Dollar Saloon in Puxico, a small town in West Texas. Puxico was several hundred miles from where the aborted train robbery had taken place, which meant it was just as far away from any known wanted posters. Ray liked it out here where he could move about freely, without the danger of running into some zealous lawman. He was nursing a drink and playing a game of "Old Sol." He would have welcomed a game of poker, but he couldn't afford it.

It wasn't supposed to be this way. If the big robbery he had planned with the Coulters had gone off as it was supposed to, he would be a rich man now. He could even afford to buy some of that railroad land he had seen advertised when he rode into town this afternoon. Why, he would've had enough to buy this very saloon if he wanted to.

His thoughts returned to the saloon. Maybe he couldn't buy it, but he did plan to rob it. He had never seen a saloon that did as much business as this one. It was the middle of the afternoon and it had been full almost all day. At first, he'd thought he might be able to wait around until a slack time, until there was no one here but the bartender and a few of the whores.

But he had been here for most of the afternoon, and there hadn't been a time when the saloon was completely empty. Now he debated whether he should wait until tonight, when everything was closing down.

The problem with waiting was that he had overheard the bartender talking earlier about taking the day's receipts over to the bank to deposit them. That meant if he was going to rob the saloon, he had better do it while the money was still there.

The bat-wing doors swung open and a man came in and stepped up to the bar. Ray looked up with only a casual interest, until he saw who it was.

It was Angus Buford!

"Let me have a whiskey," Buford said. "And leave the bottle."

"Yes, sir," the bartender replied, sliding the bottle across to him. Buford put his money down on the bar and poured himself a drink. Then he turned and looked around the room. When his eyes reached Ray, they stopped.

"Well, now," Buford said. "Look who is here."

"I . . . I don't want no trouble with you," Ray said.

"If you don't want any trouble, Kingsley, why are you here?" Buford asked.

"I was just passin' through," Ray answered.

"Too bad. You shoulda kept on going."

Ray stood up. "I seen 'em, you know," he said.

"You seen who?"

"Them two dead men on the express car. I seen 'em."

Buford laughed, a short, evil laugh. "Did you? Well, you must've tried to rob that train. I figured with bait like that, someone was goin' to try. I wish I could've seen your face when you found out there was nothin' there."

"What happened to the money?"

"What money?" Buford asked. He shook his head. "There never was any money. It was all a ruse—the guards, the express car, all of it. The real money was shipped by stagecoach."

Ray's eyes narrowed. "I don't believe you," he said. "I told you, I seen the two men you left there."

"You calling me a liar, Kingsley? I don't like being called a liar."

Ray took a deep breath. "I'm callin' you a liar, 'cause that's what you are," he said.

The others in the saloon began, slowly and quietly, to ease out of the way, leaving a clear line of fire between the two men.

Buford shook his head slowly. "You should've kept go-

ing, Kingsley. Now I'm going to have to kill you, and killin' someone always puts me off my feed.''

"Could be that I'll kill you," Kingsley suggested nervously.

"Could be, but it ain't likely," Buford replied calmly,
confidently.

Ray reached down to the table to pick up his glass of
whiskey. His hand was shaking so badly, that he had to
steady it with his other hand. He turned it up to his lips,
spilling nearly as much as he drank. Then he set the glass
down and stood there with his hand hovering over his pistol.

"I'm going to let you draw first," Buford said.

Ray's eyes narrowed, and his hand started toward his
gun. Buford's shoulder jumped and the gun was in his
hand, blazing. His bullet caught Ray in the throat and Ray,
surprised by the suddenness of it, dropped his gun unfired
and clutched at his throat. Blood spilled between his fingers
as he let out a gurgling death rattle. He fell against the table,
then rolled off, dead, before he reached the floor.

IT WAS SIX WEEKS LATER THAT WIN AND JOE walked
into the Bull's Neck Saloon in Austin, Texas, having been
summoned there by a telegraph message from Jeb Finley.

"Thank you for coming," Finley said when they joined
him at the table.

"You said you had some information that might interest
us," Win replied.

"Have you heard from Ray Kingsley?" Finley asked.

"No," Win answered. "Not since he rode off a month
or so ago."

"He's dead."

"Damn," Joe said. He sighed. "Ole Ray always was one
for gettin' his dick stuck in a crack. The law hang 'im?''

"No. He was killed by Angus Buford."

"Buford," Win snorted. "Someone should've killed that sonofabitch a long time ago."

"I know where he is, if you're interested," Finley said.

"Why would we be interested in where he is?" Win asked.

"I thought Ray Kingsley was your friend."

"He was," Win agreed. "But if we went around avenging ever'one we ever knew who got himself killed, that's all we'd be doing."

"Buford also has the money that you missed when you tried to hold up the train," Finley said. "Or quite a bit of it."

"How much of it?"

"He has bought a lot of property, but he still has over one hundred thousand dollars in cash."

"One hundred thousand?" Win said. He sighed. "That's a lot less than the amount we started out after."

"Yeah, but there are fewer of us to share now," Joe pointed out.

"Are you interested?" Finley asked.

"Yeah, we're interested," Win answered. "Where is he keeping the money . . . the cash that he has on hand?"

"I understand that he keeps it in a strongbox in his house."

"That's good to know," Win said. "That makes it a little easier to get to than if he was keepin' it in a bank."

"Where is he?" Joe asked.

Finley shook his head. "I'm not going to tell you," he said.

"What the hell do you mean you aren't going to tell us?" Win asked. "You're the one who brought it up."

"I am going to tell you, but not yet. Not before we come to some agreement."

"Wait a minute," Win said, holding out his hand. "Are you figuring on trading your information for a bigger cut of the money? Because if you are, you can just forget it. We'll find the sonofabitch without your help."

"No, I'm not asking for a larger cut. That's not it."

"Then what is it?"

"First, I need to tell you that I have just come from the governor's office," Finley said.

"The governor's office?" Joe snorted. "That's a laugh. Hell, far as I know, the people of Texas don't even have a governor. All they got is that sonofabitch the Yankee army appointed."

"Regardless of how James Throckmorton got there, he is the legal governor of the state of Texas," Finley replied. "And as governor, he has certain powers that should interest you."

"What makes you think anything Throckmorton might say or do would interest us?" Win asked.

"Because he has given me the authority, on behalf of the state of Texas, to offer you a deal," Finley replied. "Texas will give you a reward of ten percent of any and all monies you may recover from Buford and his accomplices."

"Ten percent?"

"Yes. If our information is correct, that will be approximately ten thousand dollars."

"Let me get this straight," Win said. "You're asking us to take the one hundred thousand dollars Buford has in his safe, and then give ninety thousand of it to the state of Texas?"

"Yes," Finley said.

"Why the hell would we do something like that?" Win asked.

"You would be earning not only the gratitude of the state

of Texas, but an official pardon as well," Finley said.

"Is that what this is all about, Finley?" Win asked.
"Have you gone to make a deal with the governor to get
yourself a pardon? Well, if you have, you weren't talking
for us."

"You don't understand," Finely said. "I'm not trying to
make a deal *with* Texas, I'm trying to make a deal *for*
Texas."

"For Texas? What are you talking about?"

"I am an officer of the state," Finley said.

"You are an officer of the state?"

"Yes."

Win finished his drink, then held the empty glass and
studied Finely's face for a long moment. Finally, he spoke.

"Well, I'll be damned. You've been workin' for them
all along, haven't you? I mean, even when we set this deal
up, you were working for Texas."

"Yes," Finley answered.

"You were setting us up?"

"In a manner of speaking, yes, I was," Finley admitted.

"Would you mind tellin' me who else was in on this
little scheme of yours?"

"Everyone was in on it. Everyone, that is, but you two.
And, of course, Ray Kingsley."

"Everyone?" Win asked.

Finley shook his head. "Jessica Moore, Al Santos, Christina Rawlings, Matthew Pate, and Charley Gibson. They
were all part of the plan," Finley said.

"Why did you get us involved?"

"We decided that the best time to go after the money
was when it was being transported by train. And as Al
Santos pointed out, when it comes to robbing trains, you
boys are the best."

"And what did you have in mind for us after we pulled it off?" Joe asked.

"We were going to offer you the same deal I just offered you," Finley said.

"Ten percent?" Win rolled the glass in his hands. "There were nine people involved. Just how far did you expect that ten percent to go?"

"You two and Ray Kingsley are the only ones who would have participated in the reward. The reasons the others had for being involved had very little to do with the money," Finley answered. "For example, Jessica Moore wanted to bring down the man she holds responsible for killing her father. For Matthew Pate and his daughter, it was the fact that the state of Texas was willing to forgive the back taxes on Doubletree Ranch, thus returning ownership of their ranch to them. And all Charley Gibson wanted out of it was to be reinstated as sheriff of San Saba County."

"What about you and Al? What was in it for you two?"

Finley shook his head. "Nothing but the satisfaction of doing our job. We're not eligible for anything."

"And just what is your job?"

"I'm Chief of the Governor's Special Deputy Force, and Al Santos is one of my deputies. That means the entire ten percent would have been yours. Yours and Ray Kingsley's. So you see, it would only have been split three ways. And don't forget, the amount of money we were talking about then was three hundred thousand dollars."

"Still, thirty thousand dollars split three ways is a hell of a lot less than we were led to believe we were going to get," Joe grumbled.

"I admit that, but I was taking a chance that you would see it my way," Finley said.

"What if you couldn't have talked us into coming around?" Win asked.

"If you had refused the deal I was going to arrest you and turn all the money over to the state," Finley admitted.

"Did you think we would just give up all that money without a fight?" Joe asked.

"I hoped it wouldn't have to go that far," Finley said. He sighed. "But I was prepared for it, if necessary."

"Were you also prepared to die?" Joe asked. "Because if you had tried something like that, you would've been the first one to go."

"Yes, I was prepared. And I am prepared now, if need be," Finley said.

"What do you mean you are prepared now?" Puzzled by Finley's statement, Win sensed that something wasn't quite right, and he took a quick glance around the saloon. That was when he realized that they were being very closely watched by several men who had been posing as customers at the other tables. "Damn you," Win hissed.

"I wondered how long it would take you to notice that you are surrounded," Finley said. "These are my deputies. You are both wanted men. I could take you to jail right now."

"You don't think we'd go peaceably, do you?" Joe asked.

"I don't know. I would hope so. If you put up any kind of fight at all, both of you will die."

"And some of you as well," Joe warned, menacingly.

"Yes, that's true. But don't forget, these men are also veterans, and many is the time they have gone into battle knowing that they or their friends might die. That didn't stop them then, and it won't stop them now."

"You son of a bitch!" Joe said. He started to reach for

his gun, but Win stuck his hand up quickly and stopped him.

"No, Little Brother, hold it," he said. "Finley is right. We won't accomplish a thing except a little killing." He looked at Finley. "It's your call now, Colonel."

"The offer still stands," Finley said. "Ten percent of what you recover. Also, Throckmorton has promised a full pardon."

"What good is a full pardon from the acting governor of Texas going to do us?" Joe asked. "We're a couple of Missouri boys."

"It won't do anything for you in Missouri, or Kansas, or anywhere except Texas," Finley admitted. "But at least you'll be able to ride into any Texas town without worrying about the law."

As Win was contemplating the offer, he looked again at the deputies. That was when he saw Al Santos sitting quietly, and unobtrusively, at the table nearest the door. Win nodded.

"Hello, Al."

Al nodded back. "Win, it's good to see you again," he said.

"A full pardon and ten thousand dollars?" Win said to Finley.

"Win, wait a minute!" Joe said anxiously. "You ain't thinkin' of takin' him up on the deal, are you?"

"Well, if you have a better suggestion, Little Brother, I'm open to it," Win said.

"We could hit Buford ourselves, and keep the money," Joe suggested.

"Yes, we could do that," Win agreed. He looked back at Finley and smiled. "But I sort of get the idea that if we don't agree to the terms right now, Finley and his deputies are goin' to throw us in jail."

Finley chuckled. "You've got that right. Listen, boys, you haven't stayed alive this long by being dumb. Now, don't be dumb now. Take the offer."

Joe stroked his chin as he studied those arrayed around him. Finally, he sighed in resignation. "All right, Win, it's your call," he said. "Whatever you decide, I'll go along with it."

Win looked back at Finley. "I want the full pardon for my brother and me now, before we leave town," he said.

Finley smiled, then took out two sheets of paper and handed them across the table to Win and Joe. "I thought you might want something like that," he said. "That's already been taken care of."

"And I want five hundred dollars working money," Win added. "Two hundred fifty each."

"Five hundred dollars?" Finley gasped. He shook his head. "I don't know. The governor didn't say anything about authorizing any kind of fee in advance."

Win forced a smile. "You are Chief of the Governor's Special Deputy Force. Use your influence to talk him into it."

Finley sighed, then pushed his chair back with a scrape and stood up.

"All right, it's a deal. You'll get your pardon and your five hundred dollars. Now, where will I bring the money."

"Why, with all the amenities this place has to offer?" Win replied, taking in the saloon with a sweep of his arm. "You can bring it right here. This is where we'll be."

15

After Finley and his deputies left, Win ordered dinner and drinks. The soiled doves who normally worked the saloon had moved to the back of the room while all the deputies were present, in order to be out of the line of fire if any shooting erupted. Now they began to circulate again, and seeing them, Joe caught the eye of one and smiled at her.

"Found something to stir your interest, Little Brother?" Win asked, as he transferred a piece of steak from the plate to his mouth.

"That gal over there in blue," Joe said, nodding in the girl's direction.

Chewing, Win turned to look over his shoulder. "The one in green is prettier," he said.

"Green? Well, that just shows how much you know," Joe said. "Did you see how skinny she was? It'd be like pokin' your pecker through a knothole. Besides which, if you'll just notice, that girl in green ain't even got no titties."

Win glanced back over his shoulder a second time. By now a few of the girls were aware that they were the object of the boys' contemplation, and they began preening for them.

"She's got titties," Win said. "I'll admit they aren't very big, but she's got 'em."

"Not enough for me," Joe said. "I like 'em with a little meat on their bones," he continued, "and that gal in blue is just right. Look at the size of them titties. You know, if a fella was to fall down in between 'em, he'd like as not smother before he could get hisself excavated."

Win chuckled.

"Here she comes," Joe said.

The woman in blue sauntered over to the table. Realizing she had caught Joe's fancy, she put her hands on the table and leaned forward in front of him, giving him a good show down the scoop-top of her dress.

"Do you see something you like?" she asked pointedly.

Joe, who had finished his supper, stood up. "Yeah, but I ain't seen enough of it yet," he said. He smiled. "Although I got me a feelin' you might be willin' to show me. What's your name?"

"The name's Amy," the girl answered.

"Well, Amy, how about we go upstairs?"

"You got a copper chit?" Amy asked, referring to the copper chits that were for sale at the bar, to be redeemed only for a soiled dove's favors.

"I don't have one yet," Joe said. "But I reckon I can go buy one." He stuck his hand in his pockets, searching them all, but coming up empty. When Amy saw that he was broke, she frowned and started to walk away. "No, wait!" Joe said. Joe looked at Win. "Win?"

"Damn, Joe, you're already into me for five dollars," he said.

"Yeah, but can't you see that this is a goddamn emergency?" Joe asked.

Laughing, Win took out some money and gave it to his brother. When Amy saw that Joe now had the wherewithal, she was all smiles again, and she put her arm through his.

"What about your brother?" Amy asked as they started up the stairs.

"What about him?"

"You may have noticed that I have several friends who are unengaged for the moment. Perhaps he would like to meet one of them?"

"Nah," Joe said, laughing. He motioned for her to lean over so he could whisper. "He don't like girls," he hissed.

"Oh, my!" Amy gasped, looking around in shock. "Why, I don't believe I've never actually known such a person." Quickly, she whispered the news to the other girls, who, like Amy, began to stare in curiosity at Win.

Win, who had not heard his brother's joke, continued to eat his supper, unaware of the fact that he was now the center of intense scrutiny on the part of the women.

"Hell's bells," the girl in the green dress said. "I seen the way he looked at me while ago. I'll bet I could change his mind."

WHEN JOE AND AMY REACHED THE SECOND FLOOR, AMY opened a closet door and reached in to get towels. To her consternation, she found none, so she called down to the other end of the long hall.

"Mary! Mary, where are the clean towels?"

A very stout, very plain-looking woman stepped out of a room at the other end.

"They're down here," she said. "I brought them in from the line and folded them. I just haven't got around to putting them in the closet yet. You can come down here and get them if you need any now."

"Mary, I don't want to come down there and get them,"

Amy replied sternly. "I thought we had an understanding, a division of labor, so to speak. We fuck, you keep us supplied with clean towels."

"All right," Mary said. "I'll bring some right down."

"Thank you," Amy said. She turned to Joe. "I tell you, ever since Mary came off the line she's been just real mean-spirited."

When the towels were brought, Amy took one, then putting her hand on Joe's arm, led him into one of the rooms.

THE CLOSENESS OF HER STIRRED HIM. SHE SMELLED OF woman, of sweat and musk, and when she leaned against him, her breasts lay against his arm.

Her face moved close to his, her lips pressed against his own. She flicked her tongue hotly into his mouth, explored, licked, sucked.

Joe crushed her against him, fired by his need for her.

"Wait," she panted. She broke away then and began to undress, now revealing one nipple, now concealing one, part of the art of seduction, well learned in her profession.

"You get undressed too," she whispered. "Hurry, I can't wait anymore!"

Joe stripped out of his clothes, and felt the massage of air against his naked skin. He reached for her, but she stepped back.

"What . . . ?" he said.

Amy went onto her knees in front of him, then put her hot palms against his hips. She took his cock in her long, supple fingers. "It's so beautiful," she murmured. She squeezed it gently.

Joe groaned. A silver droplet appeared on the slit of his swollen shaft.

"Oh, my," Amy whispered. Her tongue darted out,

sending a jolt of pleasure through him. The drop disappeared.

Joe groaned again.

"You taste good," she said. "I want to taste more."

Amy took a deep breath, then bent over him, taking his cock into her mouth. She moved her lips down the shaft, feeling the soft crown against her palate, flicking her tongue against the slit, tasting the fluids that seeped out. She moved her mouth up to the head, then as far back down on the shaft as she could, sliding him in and out of her mouth. Her loins churned with heat, her juices boiled and bubbled through her bush.

After a few moments of this, she released his engorged cock and began to make her way up his belly, raining tiny kisses across his muscled body.

He grabbed her in his arms, laid her on the bed, then moved on top of her, feeling her juices, which had spilled over. He had grown larger in her eager mouth, his desire more urgent.

Quickly he lowered his body onto her soft, resilient frame. She spread her legs for him, her pink vulva opening in anticipation, begging for the ultimate invasion. He slipped his cock into the oiled, velvet sheath.

Amy gasped as she felt him plunge deep inside her. She thrashed against him, making little sobbing sounds as he withdrew, slid in, then withdrew again. With a practiced motion she squeezed and massaged his shaft, milked him for his seed.

The two locked together, plunging, rising. The wet sound of flesh against oiled flesh filled the room with sound. Amy stiffened and moaned as the first wave of orgasm swept over her body. Joe continued unabated, pounding deep into her welcoming cleft. Her moans grew in intensity, becoming enraptured cries as wave upon wave of pleasure consumed her.

Joe felt himself sliding forward, and knowing that Amy had already climaxed, made no effort to hold back, but rode with it, melting and pouring out the end of his cock. The first enormous gush traveled the length of his cock and exploded into her velvet smoothness. She felt him, and gasped with the final pleasure, staying with him as his seed boiled out of his body.

Finally spent, he fell from her, breathing hard.

Later, when both had calmed down, Amy spoke.

"Why?" she asked.

"Why what?" Joe replied, wondering what she was talking about.

"Your brother," she said. "Why doesn't he like girls?"

"I don't know," Joe answered. "Crazy, I guess." He laughed at his private joke.

THE TOWN OF PUXICO WAS THREE HUNDRED MILES FROM Austin, located at what was currently the western terminus of the Texas Western Railroad. Like any boom town, it was suffering from the effects of growing too fast. Saloons, brothels, and gambling halls were being built faster than stores, schools, and churches, so that many of the town's newly arrived residents were less than desirable citizens.

Elijah Cline, owner-publisher of the *Puxico Gazette*, had lamented that fact often in his newspaper, and today he had just penned another story expressing his opinion, in which he wrote:

Have we sold ourselves for thirty pieces of silver? Have we been blinded by the glitter of gold? My friends, if we are truthful we must admit that the answer to these questions is "yes."

The good citizens of this town have watched with dismay as bordellos replaced boardinghouses, saloons pushed away family businesses, and gambling halls supplanted churches. We have suffered an influx of humanity as new arrivals have come, not to build, but to destroy. The very dregs of society have found their way to Puxico. Our streets are filled with drunken and debased men and women who have no regard for decency, nor respect for the rights of others.

And what is the cause of this slide toward Gomorrah? Some might say that such growing pangs are experienced by any town that is touched by the railroad. But I strongly disagree with that notion. Hundreds, nay, thousands of cities and towns all across the country have watched the railroad arrive and have benefited greatly from it. Are we to believe that the good citizens of Puxico are of such poor stock that they cannot handle what others have handled?

No, I do not believe that. It is not the railroad that has brought such distress to our community. It is the nefarious dealings of one man. One man who has burst upon the scene with thousands upon thousands of dollars which he has spread in such a way as to generate vice and corruption, the better to gain total and absolute control, not only of our business and economy, but of our very souls.

He has acquired enough land through distress sales to start a ranch he calls the ''Rocking L.'' The Rocking L has become little more than a haven for desperadoes and outlaws. We have all seen them, the ill-mannered bullies who crowd the decent citizens off the sidewalks, and think nothing of making public displays of their drunkenness and boorish behavior.

It is no secret why the Rocking L would hire such

men, for it seems more than mere coincidence that the herd of cows at the Rocking L ranch is experiencing a growth rate commensurate with the degree of loss in all the other herds of the county. And when neighboring ranchers have made a friendly request to peruse Rocking L land for cattle that may have "strayed," they are denied that access by the armed intervention of those same outlaws and desperadoes with which the Rocking L is peopled.

How did one man come by so much money that he is able to spend it so freely? Those who have earned money honestly, by the sweat of their brow or the fruits of their labor, are much more discriminating in their spending and investments. It has been my experience that only ill-gotten gains are disposed of in such a cavalier fashion as is the case I have brought before you today.

I think it is time that the owner of the Rocking L be thoroughly investigated. We should know the source of his wealth, the better to be able to judge his intentions. And we should unite to pass laws and ordinances that will greatly inhibit his ability to destroy our town.

Cline lifted the first copy of today's edition from the platen of the Washington Hand Press, and held it up, the fresh ink glistening black on the page. There was something about a newly printed newspaper, something that stirred the blood and made him want to shout out in pride.

The newspaper in Puxico was the third Cline had published. With a burning zeal to be a journalist and a heavy freight wagon, he had loaded up press, type, imposing tones, ink, and paper to come West. The other two towns had seemed indifferent to a newspaper. Here in Puxico, however, he was actually beginning to make a profit.

But now he felt that all he and the other decent citizens of Puxico had worked for was being endangered by the actions of a very wealthy, ambitious, and ruthless man who, though only recently arrived, was taking control of the town and of everyone who chose to live there. He had made the decision, therefore, to do what he could to alert the citizens of the town to the danger that had so recently come into their midst.

"They say the pen is mightier than the sword," he said to himself as he looked over his page. "I guess we're about to find out."

Cline printed another two hundred copies of the paper, then carried them out with him, leaving them at locations about town where merchants agreed to sell his papers for him. One such place was the Silver Dollar Saloon. There, he left a stack of fifty papers, picked up four left over from the day before, took forty-six cents from a bowl where people left their money to pay for the paper, then walked back out onto the street to continue his rounds.

AT ABOUT THE SAME TIME ELIJAH CLINE WAS MAKING HIS rounds, Peterson and McCloud were riding up to a house at the edge of town which belonged to a man named John Minner. Peterson swung down from his horse, while McCloud remained mounted.

The house was small and unpainted, but the front yard was ablaze with summer flowers carefully planted and tended by Mrs. Minner. On the side of the house a garden of lettuce, tomatoes, beans, corn, squash, and potatoes flourished.

"That's far enough, Peterson," a man's voice said, and John Minner stepped through the front door, carrying a long Civil War rifle in his hands. Behind him, peering tentatively out the door, was his wife, a handsome woman in her late thirties.

Peterson stopped when Minner called to him.

"Mr. Minner, no need of you actin' like that," he said. "I come out here to make you a business proposition. Mr. Lane wants to buy your store, and he is willing to pay a fair price for it."

"I know what his offer is," Minner said. "And I ain't interested in takin' it."

Peterson sighed, took off his hat, and mopped his sweating forehead.

"It's hot, Mr. Minner. Too hot to be standin' out here in the sun talkin' about this. Couldn't we discuss it inside?"

"No need. We got nothin' to discuss. Now you and that fella with you just get on out of here. I see you comin' up my walk again, I won't be so friendly."

Peterson smiled, and tried a joke. "Why, Mr. Minner, do you call this friendly?"

"I didn't shoot you on sight, mister. That's as friendly as you're goin' to get from me."

Peterson sighed, then started back toward his horse. He climbed on, then took the reins from McCloud.

"Mr. Minner, I wish you had been more cooperative than this. Our partner is very anxious to own your store, and I believe he will get it one way or the other."

"He don't really want my store atall," Minner said. "The only reason he wants to buy it is so he can close it and charge folks a lot more for goods they'll be forced to buy at his store."

"Business is business, Minner," Peterson said.

IN PUXICO TWO DAYS LATER, THE HOMES, SCHOOLS, churches, stores, saloons, brothels, and gambling halls were abuzz with the story of two fires in one night. John and

Mary Minner had been found inside their house, burned to death.

Normally, the story of two fires in one night would be front page news. But because the *Puxico Gazette* was the other building that had been destroyed that night, there was no newspaper to carry the story. And like John and Mary Minner, Elijah Cline had been found dead in the smoking embers of his rooms, which were located over the newspaper office.

16

WHEN WIN AND JOE COULTER ARRIVED IN PUXICO, THEY looked around at a community where false-fronted shanties and substantial two-story buildings competed with canvas tents for space along both sides of the street. The town was noisy with the sound of hammering and sawing, while half a dozen vehicles of commerce creaked up and down the street. So industrious was the town that two recently burned buildings were already being cleared out, their charred remains being loaded onto wagons that were backed up to the now-empty lots.

"You sure this is the right place?" Joe asked, as the two brothers rode by one of the burned-out buildings.

"You saw the sign outside of town same as I did," Win answered. "It said Puxico, and that's where Finley said we'd find Buford."

"I'll give the town this," Joe said. "It sure as hell is a busy little place."

"Yeah, it is at that," Win said. He pointed to the Silver Dollar Saloon. "What do you say we start our search in here?"

"That's the best idea you've had all day," Joe said. "I

really need a drink. My mouth's got enough dust to plant a field of corn.''

Though it was still mid-afternoon, the saloon was already crowded and noisy with the sounds of idle men and painted women having fun. Near the piano three men and a couple of women filled the air with their idea of a song, the lyrics a bit more ribald than the composer had intended.

''Yes, sir, what can I do for you boys?'' the bartender asked, sliding down toward them. He was wearing a stained apron and carrying a towel he used to alternately wipe off the bar, then wipe out the glasses.

''What's your whiskey?'' Win asked.

''Got some Old Overholt. Cost you two dollars the bottle or ten cents the drink.''

''Leave the bottle,'' Win said, slapping the necessary silver on the counter.

The bartender put the bottle and a couple of glasses on the bar, and Joe began to pour.

''You boys just passin' through?'' the bartender asked.

''Could be,'' Win said. ''Or it could be that we might stay for a while. This looks like a pretty live town.''

The bartender chuckled. ''Yes, sir, it's that, all right,'' he said. ''It started growin' when the railroad come through here. Then a month or so ago, a big investor from the East arrived. He bought up several smaller spreads and built the Rocking L, a big ranch just outside of town. And he started spreadin' his money aroun' buyin' up old businesses, building' new ones. He has caused the town to really boom.''

''Who is this man that's throwin' around all that money?'' Win asked, lifting his glass.

''A fella by the name of Lane,'' the bartender replied. ''Some says he's a carpetbagger, but if so, I got no complaints.'' The bartender made a motion with his hand. ''As you can see, his bein' here sure has been good for my business."

"I reckon so," Win agreed. "Lane, you say? You sure that's his name?"

"Well, sir, all I know is, that's the name he's goin' by. Buford Lane."

"Buford!" Joe said.

"Yeah, I know," Win answered with a nod. He tossed down a drink.

"You know him?" the bartender asked.

"Could be that we know him," Win said. "Is Lane a big man with a puffy nose and blue eyes?"

"That's him, all right," the bartender said. "He's just bought a ranch and word is he's hirin' hands, if you boys is lookin' for work."

"We might be," Win said. "How do we find him?"

"The place he bought is just west of town," the bartender said. "You can't miss it. It's a two-story white house, with a huge cottonwood tree in the front yard."

"Well, as I live and breathe, if it ain't Win and Joe Coulter!" a voice suddenly said.

Surprised to be recognized here, Win and Joe turned to see who had hailed them. A big, bearded man, with a wide smile on his face, was coming toward them with his hand extended. "Never thought I'd run into you two boys way out here," he said. "I thought you was going to stay in Missouri and farm."

"Tom Malloy," Win said, recognizing a man who had ridden with them when they were with Quantrill. "How've you been?"

"Been stayin' out of trouble," Malloy said. He laughed. "Or stayin' out of town when I couldn't stay out of trouble. Say, did you boys hear about Ray Kingsley? He got hisself shot down right here in this very saloon." Malloy lowered his voice, then looked around. "Ever'one's sayin' it was a fair fight," he said. "But the fella that shot 'im, this here Buford Lane, purt' near owns the town from what I can find out, so what would you expect ever'one to say. Even if ole' Ray had a chance . . . he never really had a chance."

"What are you doing out here, Tom?" Joe asked.

"Tryin' to get as far away from all those Yankee carpetbaggin' bastards as I can," Malloy answered. "I bought a train ticket, but this is as far west as the railroad would take me. So this mornin' I bought a good horse and now I'm playin' a little cards, tryin' to raise enough of a stake to go on to California. Say, what about you two boys? You want to go to California with me? They say it's mighty fine country out there."

"We may get out there some day," Win said.

"But we got a little business to take care of here first," Joe added.

"Malloy!" someone called from a nearby table. "We're about to deal a new hand. You in or not?"

"I'm in," Malloy said, starting back toward the table and the other players. He stopped and looked back toward Win and Joe. "Listen, if you boys ever get out California way, look me up."

"We'll do that," Win promised.

AT ANOTHER TABLE ONE OF THE PLAYERS STARTED PICKing up his money. "Deal me out, boys," he said.

"You sure you don't want to stick around for a few more hands? Your luck might change," one of the other players said.

"Not today, I'm afraid. I'll see you boys later."

As he was leaving, someone from the bar came over to take his seat and the game continued, his absence barely noticed by the other players.

The player who abandoned the game was Mitchell McCloud, and as McCloud left the saloon he looked over his shoulder toward the bar and the two men he had heard identified as Win and Joe Coulter. He was certain Buford would be interested in this bit of information.

"YOU'RE SURE IT WAS THEM?" BUFORD ASKED AS HE LIT his cigar.

"I was as close to 'em then as I am to that settee over there now," McCloud said. "And I heard 'em talkin' as plain as if they was talkin' to me. A fella called 'em by name. Win and Joe Coulter, he said. And then they started talkin' like they'd know'd each other for a long time."

"Well, I'll give 'em this," Buford said. "They sure don't give up easy."

"Maybe they're just passin' through," Peterson suggested. The three men were in the parlor of Buford's ranch house, having gone in there to discuss the news McCloud had brought them from town.

"No," Buford answered. "If they're in Puxico, they've come for the money."

"What are we goin' to do about it?" Peterson asked.

"Do? I'll tell you what *you* are going to do. You two are going to kill them," Buford said, easily.

"What do you mean, we are going to kill them?" McCloud asked. "What about you?"

"They know me," Buford said. "They've never seen either of you, so it would be much easier for you to do it than it would me. And don't forget, you have as much at stake in this as I do."

"Not quite as much," Peterson said. "You've got most of it now."

"It is not my fault that I have invested my money wisely,

whereas you two have squandered most of yours on gambling, whiskey, and women."

"Which you let us do, since you now own most of the saloons, gambling halls, and whorehouses," McCloud grumbled.

"I'm not your keeper," Buford said.

"And we're not your soldiers anymore. You can't just send us out to kill the way you could during the war."

Buford looked at the two of them for a moment, then sighed. "All right," he said. "Why don't I make it worth your while? I'll give you ten thousand dollars to kill them, five thousand dollars for each of you. But you must kill both of them."

Peterson and McCloud looked at each other, then nodded.

"Hell," Peterson said, answering for both of them. "For ten thousand dollars I'd kill my own mother."

WHEN BUFORD WENT BACK UPSTAIRS JESSICA MOORE WAS waiting for him, lying naked on the bed. Her legs were splayed so that she was displaying herself: open, pink, and glistening through the nest of pubic hair.

"What took you so long?" she asked. She put her hand just above her knee, drew it up the long, fleshy thigh, then let her fingers slide through the slit, where they lingered for a moment before moving up her stomach, across her breasts with the taut nipples, then to her lips. She sucked her fingers pointedly.

"It was nothing," Buford said. "Just a little business to take care of, that's all."

"You haven't forgotten, have you, that you have some business to take care of here?"

Buford began to get out of his clothes. "I've never

known a woman like you," he said, as he started toward the bed.

"Like me? How like me?"

"Always ready to fuck. Are you like that with every man you meet?"

Jessica smiled. "No, not with every man. Just with men who have what it takes to excite me."

"You mean this?" Buford asked, grabbing himself now and showing her his erection.

"Well, that too," she said.

"That too?" Buford asked, puzzled by her comment. "What do you mean that too? What else?"

"Money," she said candidly. "You have become a very wealthy man, Angus Buford. And as you have no doubt noticed, I like to fuck wealthy men."

"You never really let that fat-assed bastard fuck you, did you?"

"Are you talking about General Bellefontaine?" Jessica asked.

"Yes. Did you really let him fuck you?"

"I let him try," she said. "But he was old and fat, and he couldn't do it very well." She smiled. "That's why I helped you get the money."

"You weren't all that much help. All you did was give me the combination to the vault," Buford said.

"If I hadn't you would have never gotten the money," she said.

"What about Win Coulter?"

"What about him?" Jessica asked. The smile left her face.

"Did you let him fuck you?"

Jessica pasted the smile back on, and reached for him. "You talk too much," she said. She pulled him toward her, then wrapped her legs around his waist to facilitate his entry.

Jessica felt him move into her, felt his hands cover her breasts. As always, he began without tenderness, without preliminaries, without any regard as to how she might feel, or what she might want. That was why she had adopted an attitude of sexual aggression. She was able to derive her sexual pleasure not from anything Angus Buford did for her, but from the control she was able to exercise over him.

It had not been that way with Win Coulter. She had initiated sex with him, but once it began, he'd taken the initiative from her. He'd become the aggressor, and she his willing victim. With Win Coulter, she had discovered sexual pleasures unlike any she had ever experienced before, and it had frightened her. Frightened her because she knew that with Win Coulter, she would never again be in control.

It was the fear of losing control that had made her change her plans about Bellefontaine's money. When she returned to San Saba, she went to Angus Buford and offered to provide him with the combination to the vault. He accepted her offer, and the theft went off as planned, though she had not realized that he was going to kill her brother and the poor accountant.

Part of her reason for doing this was to get revenge on Bellefontaine, and in this she had been successful, for Bellefontaine lost everything. He even lost his ranches when the courts heard the lawsuits filed by Matthew Pate and the other ranchers, and ruled that the confiscation of their land for non-payment of taxes had been improperly handled.

Bellefontaine left San Saba a broken and discredited man. So complete was his fall from the pinnacle that Jessica almost felt sorry for him as he started the long trip back to Kansas.

Jessica then came to Puxico to claim her share. It had been her intention to take the money and go somewhere to start a new life, but Buford told her that he had very little cash remaining, having invested it all in land and business deals.

"Give me six months and you'll have your share three times over," he promised.

Under the circumstances, Jessica had no choice. She accepted his offer. In the meantime, she planned to protect her interest by doing everything she could do to make him sexually dependent upon her.

And right now, as he groaned and thrust and grunted above her, she knew that that part of her plan was working perfectly.

17

AT THE SUPPER TABLE IN KATHY'S RESTAURANT, JOE ordered a second piece of pie. "What about you, Win?" he asked. "Don't you want some pie?"

"I had a piece already," Win said.

"Well, yeah, so did I, but what difference does that make?"

Win laughed. "It means I'm full. I can't hold another bite."

"God, Big Brother, I never knew what a poor appetite you had," Joe said, smiling in anticipation as a second generous slice of apple pie was put before him.

Win stood up.

"Aren't you going to wait around?" Joe asked.

"And watch you eat? No, thank you," Win answered. "I think I'll go over to the stable and check on the horses. If we're going to go out there, we need to do it tonight, before anyone gets wind of what we're about."

"Good idea. I'll be ready to go soon's I finish this."

AS WIN STEPPED OFF THE BOARDWALK IN FRONT OF THE restaurant, a bullet suddenly fried the air just beside his ear, hit the dirt beside him, then skipped off with a high-pitched whine down the street. The sound of the rifle shot reached him at about the same time, and Win dropped and rolled to his left, his gun already in his hand. That was when he saw the rifleman standing on the porch roof of the general store, just behind the "Dunnigan's Finest Selections" sign. The would-be assailant was operating the lever, chambering in another round, when Win fired. Win's shot flew true, and he saw the rifle drop to the ground as the ambusher grabbed his throat, then pitched forward, turning a half-flip in the air to land flat on his back. A little puff of dust rose from the impact of his falling body.

Another gunman appeared in the street at that same moment, firing at Win. But Win, with the instinct of survival, had rolled to his right after his first shot. As a result, the gunman's bullet crashed harmlessly into the wooden porch in front of the cafe.

From his prone position on the ground, Win fired at the new gunman and hit him in the knee. The gunman let out a howl and went down. He was still firing, however, and Win felt a bullet tear through the crown of his hat.

INSIDE THE RESTAURANT, JOE HAD JUST FINISHED HIS PIE when he heard the shooting. He didn't have to ask what was going on. He knew instinctively that his brother was involved, and he stood up and started for the door, checking his own pistol as he did so.

WIN THREW ANOTHER SHOT TOWARD THE GUNMAN, BUT as his attacker was lying in the street now, he made a more difficult target.

"McCloud! McCloud! Are you dead?" the gunman lying in the street shouted.

There was no answer.

Not knowing if there was anyone else after him, Win got up and ran three buildings down the street, bending low and firing as he went. He dived behind the porch of the barbershop, then rose to look back toward his attacker.

His attacker had also managed to get out of the street, and now he fired at Win. The bullet sent splinters of wood into Win's face, and Win put his hand up, then pulled it away, peppered with his own blood.

"Listen to me!" the gunman shouted. "This here fella is a murderer! There's wanted posters out on him all over East Texas! I'll give a thousand dollars to anyone who helps me kill the sonofabitch!"

"You do your own killin', Peterson!" someone shouted back. "A thousand dollars don't mean shit to a dead man!"

Win stared across the street, trying to find an opening for a shot, but Peterson, as he now knew the man's name was, had managed to crawl behind a wooden bench.

Suddenly Win smiled. Peterson had improved his position by getting out of the street and behind a wooden bench, all right, but it was in front of a dressmaker's shop. And what Peterson didn't realize was that the large mirror in the window of the dressmaker's shop showed his reflection.

From across the street, Win watched in the mirror as Peterson inched along on his belly to the far end of the bench. Win took slow and deliberate aim at the end of the bench where he knew Peterson's face would appear.

Slowly, Peterson peered around the corner of the bench to see where Win was and what was going on. Win cocked his pistol and waited. When enough of Peterson's head was exposed to give him a target, Win squeezed the trigger. His pistol roared and bucked in his hand. A cloud of smoke billowed up, then floated away. When the cloud cleared, Win saw Peterson lying face-down in the dirt with a pool of blood spreading out from under his head.

Win heard someone running toward him then, and he swung around ready, if need be, to take on someone else. When he saw that it was Joe, he smiled in relief, then stood up. Joe joined him, and the two brothers, with pistols drawn, moved to the middle of the street, then looked around with experienced eyes, searching the roofs and corners of buildings for any more adversaries. They saw several people looking at them from positions of hiding, but no one seemed threatening.

"You people!" Win called out, putting his gun away and taking out a piece of paper. "These two men were wrong! I am not a wanted man! This paper is signed by the governor of Texas, and it is a full and unconditional pardon. There's no future in anyone trying to take us on. You're either going to wind up dead, like these two . . . or if you get lucky and kill us . . . you will have risked your lives for nothing!"

"Even if you was wanted, I ain't lookin' for no bounty from a Yankee governor," someone said. Win recognized the voice as the same one who had refused Peterson's offer of a thousand dollars to help kill him. "I'm comin' out, mister, and I ain't plannin' on doin' no shootin'."

"Come ahead," Win said.

When the first man came out and nothing happened, another came out, and another still, until soon the street was once again filled. Only this time, they weren't as much pedestrians as they were spectators, for the crowd divided into two groups, half gathered around McCloud's body and the other half around Peterson's.

The sheriff came toward Win and Joe, holding his hands out in front of him to show that he had no intention of going for his gun.

"I saw the fight," he said. "Those two men attacked you, and you had no choice but to defend yourselves. But if you don't mind, I'll just have a look at that pardon you're carryin'. If it's real, I'll start sendin' out wires tomorrow to make certain any dodgers as might be out on you are pulled.''

"And if it isn't real?" Joe asked.

The sheriff stopped in his tracks and a flicker of fear passed across his face. Joe laughed.

"My brother was teasing you," Win said, holding the pardon out for the sheriff's examination. "As you can see, this is real."

The sheriff looked at it for a moment, then handed it back. "It looks genuine, all right," he said. "I'll do what I can about getting the dodgers pulled."

"Thanks," Win said. "By the way, Sheriff, do you know either of these men? You have any idea why they would try to kill me?"

"I reckon they were after the reward money," the sheriff said. "They probably didn't know about the pardon."

Win shook his head. "No," he said. "That couldn't be it. They weren't after any reward money."

"Why do you think that?"

"Because I heard this one offer a thousand dollars to anyone who would help him kill me," Win said. "And even if the dodgers were still in effect, the reward was only for five hundred dollars. Why would he be willing to pay double that?"

The sheriff shook his head. "You've got me," he said. "But then, I don't really know these fellas all that well. They came into town the same time as Lane did. As a matter of fact, I think they even worked for him. I know they always seemed to have money to spend. Not as much as Buford Lane, but enough to visit the saloons and whorehouses about every night."

"They worked for Buford?" Joe asked.

"Buford Lane, yes, they worked for him," the sheriff said.

Win and Joe looked at each other.

"So much for our surprise, Little Brother," Win said. "He already knows we are here."

18

IT HAD JUST GROWN DARK ENOUGH TO LIGHT THE LANterns when a rider galloped into the front yard on a horse that was lathered from its exertion.

"Damn," Buford said, walking over to the window to pull the curtain to one side.

"What is it?" Jessica asked.

"I'm not sure. But something sure as hell is up." Buford took his pistol belt off the hall-tree and strapped it on. Then he put on his hat and stepped outside. Several of his ranch hands, drawn by the galloping arrival of the rider, were also drifting toward the front yard to see what was going on.

"Mr. Lane," the rider called.

"Yes," Buford replied from the dark recesses of the front porch. He came out of the shadows to stand on the steps so he could be seen.

"I come to tell you," the rider said. "That is, I thought you might want to know."

"Know what, man?"

"Your two friends? Peterson and McCloud? They was both killed this evenin'," the rider said.

"Kilt?" one of the ranch hands said. "How?"

"They was killed by a stranger, a fella named Coulter, I think it was."

"Coulter!" Jessica gasped from the shadows behind Buford. "Win Coulter? He's here?"

"Go on back inside, Jessica," Buford ordered. "This doesn't concern you."

"Oh, yes, it does concern me," Jessica said. "Don't forget, I'm the one who got Win Coulter involved in the first place."

"I'm not likely to forget. But that was before," Buford said sternly. "Now I'm telling you, go back inside!"

Jessica started to speak again, but the snarling anger in Buford's voice frightened her, so she said nothing more.

Buford looked around at the men who had gathered, mostly from curiosity, in the front yard.

"Men," he said. "The ones who killed Peterson and McCloud are bushwhackers! Their names are Win and Joe Coulter, and during the war, while riding with Quantrill, they burned nearly a hundred farmhouses, almost always killing the innocent men and women they found there. I fought against 'em during the war, so now they're after me. I'm goin' to be askin' for your help."

"I don't know, Mr. Lane," one of the men replied. "I'm the first to admit that the war's over, and I ain't holdin' it ag'in you none that you fought for the Yankees. But if there's some sort of a grudge still goin' on between you and these here brothers, don't know as I've any right to mix in."

Buford knew that the man had fought for the South in the war, seeing duty at Antietam, Gettysburg, and elsewhere.

"Slater, these boys aren't like you and me. We were honorable soldiers in an honorable army. These boys were little more than outlaws, using the flag of the Confederacy as a means to rob, kill, and burn.''

"He might be right, Slater," one of the other hands said. "You seen their pictures on the posters. Hell, we all have. They were without honor. There's no way you could call such men real soldiers.''

"Still, whatever's goin' on between you, it ain't our fight," Slater said.

"I'd be willing to pay one hundred dollars to any man who would make it his fight," Buford offered.

"Do you mean one hundred dollars a man?" one of the cowboys wanted to know.

"That's what I mean. One hundred dollars to each and every one of you," Buford said. "Plus a bounty of five hundred dollars for each of the Coulter brothers, payable to whoever actually gets one of them.''

"Five hundred?" Slater asked, astounded by the figure.

"For each brother," Buford said. "And since there are two of them, that's a thousand dollars.''

"Yahoo! Let's go!" one of the men shouted. "Let's go get the bastards!''

At the shout, several of the men hurried out to the stable to saddle their horses.

It took nearly ten minutes for those who were going to get saddled and ready to ride. Finally they were ready to go, and Buford stood on the front porch, lighted now by the flickering torches carried by the riders. "All right, men," he said. "You know who you are after and you know what it's worth if you succeed. Go find them! And when you do, bring them back to me." Buford paused to take a deep breath, then added, "Dead!''

Several of the men let out a yell and nearly two dozen horsemen started out at a gallop.

•   •   •

THE RIDERS GALLOPED UNTIL THEIR BLOOD COOLED, THEIR enthusiasm waned, and their horses grew tired. Then Slater realized they were just running with no sense of direction or purpose. He pulled up, and because he was at the front of the pack, the others came to a halt with him.

"What is it? What's goin' on?" someone asked.

"Yeah, why did we stop?"

"Well, hell, fellas," Slater said. "We can't just go runnin' aroun' out here like chickens with our heads cut off. We got to have some idea of what we're doin' and where we're goin'. Else we're just wastin' time and wearin' out horses."

"Well, what now?" one of the other riders asked. "I mean, I ain't flatterin' myself that I'm the one who'll get the thousand dollars. But I ain't ready to just give up on the hundred we'll all get if somebody else gets them."

"We gotta have someone in charge," Slater said.

"You do it," someone called.

"Yeah, Slater, you take charge. For a hundred dollars, we'll even listen to you." The others laughed nervously.

"All right, then," Slater said. "We're going to divide up. About three or four of you go with each group. That way we can spread out and cover more territory."

"What do we do if we find them?" someone asked.

"If you find them and you kill them, then your group can divide up the thousand dollars among you," Slater said.

"Yeah, yeah, that's for me," someone said. "I'm for killin' the sonsabitches and takin' the money."

Within a moment there were as many as five small groups, fanning out in all different directions. Now that they had a sense of direction and purpose, their enthusiasm returned.

• • •

WIN AND JOE COULTER SAW A LITTLE GROUP OF MEN COM-
ing after them. They were sitting calmly on top of a large
round rock, watching, as four riders approached a narrow
draw. The draw was so confined that the riders would not
be able to get through without squeezing down into a single
file. It was a place that no one with any tactical sense would
go into, but these were not men with a sense of tactics.
These were cowboys, fired up by the promise of a hundred-
dollar reward just for searching, and another thousand for
bringing in the Coulters dead. There wasn't one of them
who wouldn't pull the trigger on Win or Joe if they had
the opportunity. Because of that, they were men who could
be easily lured into a trap.

Win stood up so he could clearly be seen.

"Win!" Joe hissed. "What are you doing?"

"Setting the trap," Win replied easily.

"Look!" one of the approaching riders shouted.
"There's one of them!"

"They're up there!"

"Come on! Let's get them! Let's get the sonsabitches!"

The riders galloped through the draw, bent on capturing
or killing the Coulter brothers, or at least the one they had
spotted.

A couple of the men in front thought that Win made an
easy target, so they pulled their pistols and began

Win could see the flash of the gunshots, then the little
puffs of dust as the bullets hit far short. The spent bullets
whined as they ricocheted on by him, though none of the
missiles came close enough to cause him to duck.

Almost casually, Win pulled two homemade torpedoes
from his saddlebags and lit the fuses. His elevated position
allowed him to, quite easily, drop the blasting charges at
each end of the draw. The first explosion went off about
fifty yards in front of the lead rider. It was a heavy, stom-

ach-shaking thump that filled the draw with smoke and dust, then brought a ton of rocks crashing down to close the draw so the riders couldn't get through.

The second explosion, which was somewhat less powerful, was tossed behind the riders, bringing the rocks crashing down into the draw behind them, and closing the passage. Win chuckled.

"It's going to be a while before those boys are able to dig themselves out of there," he said.

Win and Joe scrambled down from the rock, then wriggled through a fissure that was just large enough to allow them to pass through. They had left their horses on the other side, and now they mounted, leaving the trapped cowboys behind them.

They rode no more than a quarter of a mile before they saw the next group of riders. Attracted by the sounds of the explosions and the gunshots, they were hurrying over to see what was happening.

"There they are!" one of the riders shouted when he spotted Win and Joe.

"Get them!" another yelled.

Win and Joe headed into a mesquite thicket. The limbs slapped painfully against their faces and arms, but on the positive side, the thicket closed behind them, hiding them from view.

"Joe, lead my horse and keep going!" Win shouted. He hopped down and gave the reins to Joe, who continued to ride.

After Joe rode off, Win squatted behind a mesquite bush and waited.

In less than ten seconds, their pursuers came by. Win waited until the first three had passed before he made his move. Then he reached up and grabbed the fourth rider and jerked him off his horse. The man gave a short, startled cry as he was going down, but the cry was cut off when he broke his neck in the fall.

The rider just ahead heard the cry, and he looked around in time to see what was happening.

"Hey! They're back here!" he called. The rider had been riding with his pistol in his hand, so he was able to get off a shot at almost the same moment he yelled.

The man was either a much better shot than Win had anticipated or he was lucky, for the bullet grazed the fleshy part of Win's arm, not close enough to make a hole, but close enough to cut a deep, painful crease. The impact of the bullet, plus the effort of unseating the rider, caused Win to go down and he fell on his right side, thus preventing him from getting to his gun. The shooter had no such constraints, however, and he was able to get off a second shot. This time his bullet hit a mesquite limb right in front of Win's face, and would have hit Win had the limb not been there. Win knew now that the first shot had not been a lucky accident. This man could shoot.

Win rolled hard, not only to be able to get out of the line of fire, but also to be able to reach his gun. As he pulled his gun up in front of him, though, he saw that it was filled with dirt. He couldn't pull the trigger—if he did, the thing might explode.

The cowboy, seeing that Win's gun was clogged, smiled in triumph and raised his pistol for a slow, carefully aimed shot. Win braced himself for it, staring helplessly at the big black hole in the end of the barrel.

Suddenly another shot rang out and Win saw the shooter grab his chest, then pitch backward off his horse. At that moment Joe rode up, the gun in his hand still smoking. He turned toward the other two riders, and they, suddenly realizing that the odds were now even, fired once, then turned and galloped away.

Though the shots were just thrown in the direction of Win and Joe, one of them managed to clip the reins to Win's horse, and the animal, suddenly free, bolted away, leaving Joe holding a severed piece of rein in his hand.

"Damn!" Joe said.

"Never mind, I'll take this one," Win shouted, leaping onto the horse of the man Joe had just shot.

With both brothers mounted, they began tracking Win's horse down, only to discover that one of the other groups had already found it. The cowboys had dismounted, and were giving their own horses a rest. One of the riders was taking a drink from a canteen, another was leaning up against a rock holding their horses, the third was examining Win's horse, and the fourth was standing a short distance away relieving himself.

Win and Joe dismounted and sneaked up closer on foot.

"It's got to be one of their horses," one of the men said. "It sure don't belong to Lane."

"How do you know?"

"It don't have the Rocking L brand."

"Hell, what's that mean?" one of the other men asked, laughing. "Half the animals on this ranch don't have the Rocking L brand. And them that do has it burned across another brand."

"You sayin' Mr. Lane rustles?"

"Let's just say he throws a wide loop." The others laughed. "Hell, we all do," he went on. "Else we wouldn't be workin' here. Why do you think he pays us double what any other rancher pays?"

"Arnie, what the hell you doin' over there anyway?" one of the men asked of the one who was relieving himself.

"What's it look like I'm doin'?" Arnie answered. "I'm watterin' the lilies."

"Goddammit, you been pissin' for five minutes. At this

rate you could hire yourself out as a fire engine.''

The others laughed.

Arnie came back toward the others, buttoning his pants. He nodded toward the horse. ''What do you say we back-track this horse and see if we can find which one of them Coulters it belonged to?''

''Hell, what difference does it make which one it belonged to?''

'' 'Cause I figure whichever one it is is most likely dead or wounded now. Probably wounded.''

''Why do you think wounded?''

'' 'Cause if he was dead, we'd know it by now. Whoever kilt him would be whoopin' and hollerin' to beat bloody hell, claimin' the extra five hundred dollars. And if he wasn't wounded, we wouldn't have his horse.''

''All right, so if we find him, what about the other one?''

''I figure they'll be together. One brother ain't goin' to leave the other. This way we got us a chance of gettin' 'em both.''

''You want both of us? We're here,'' Joe said, suddenly stepping out into the clearing.

''Goddamn! Where'd you come from?'' Arnie asked, surprised by the sudden appearance.

''I'll ask the questions,'' Win said. ''Where's Buford?'' Both he and Joe had the drop on the four men.

''We ain't tellin' you nothin','' Arnie growled.

Win squeezed off a shot, and a little mist of blood sprayed out from the side of Arnie's head. Arnie let out a yelp of pain, and interrupted his draw to slap his hand against the source of his wound.

''You son of a bitch!'' he shouted in pain and anger. ''You shot off my ear!''

''You've got one ear left,'' Win replied calmly. ''I'll let you keep it if you answer my question. Where is Buford?''

"I don't know!" Arnie grumbled.

Win popped off another shot, and the bullet took away the lobe of his other ear.

"He's back at the house!" Arnie moaned in pain. "That's all I know!"

Win lowered his pistol. "All right," he said. "Take your guns out of the holsters and empty the loads onto the ground."

The men did as they were directed.

"You," Win said, pointing to the man nearest his horse. "Bring my horse over."

The man obliged, and Win took the reins from him, then looked at the other four horses. "Let go of their reins," he ordered.

Again his instructions were followed.

Win fired a couple of shots into the dirt near the horses. The animals reared up in fright, then galloped off, their hooves clattering loudly on the rocky ground.

"Hey! What'd you do that for?" Arnie asked. "It's a long walk back."

"It's going to be longer," Win said.

"What do you mean?"

"Take off your boots."

"What? Are you crazy? I ain't givin' you my boots."

"You can walk without boots or crawl without feet," Win said dryly. "And I don't give a damn which it is." He cocked his pistol again and aimed it at the feet of one of the men.

"No, wait! Arnie, shut up! This crazy sonofabitch will do what he says!" one of the men shouted in alarm.

"All right, you can have the boots," Arnie said. He sat down and began pulling off his boots. The others joined him.

Joe collected the boots, then walked over to the horse

Win had borrowed. He tied the boots to the saddle of that horse, slapped him on the rump, and set him running.

"Goddammit! Horse, come back here! Come back here, horse!" one of the men shouted at the galloping animal.

Win and Joe mounted their own horses. Then Joe looked at the four bootless men and laughed.

"You boys walk just real careful now, you hear?" he teased. "There's not only rocks and cactus needles out there. You might also want to look out for rattlers. I hear tell they like stinkin' feet." He wrinkled his nose. "And believe you me, you boys do have stinkin' feet."

Joe laughed uproariously at his own joke as he and Win rode away, leaving the four cursing cowboys behind them.

19

WHEN BUFORD SAW SLATER RIDING INTO THE FRONT YARD later that night, he hurried out of the house to meet him.

"Did you get them?" Buford asked. "Did you kill the sonsabitches?"

"Not yet," Slater replied, swinging down from his horse.

"Where are the others? Are they still looking for them?"

"I reckon some of them are. Leastwise, the ones that ain't been killed yet," Slater answered. He started toward the bunkhouse. "That is, the ones who ain't got enough sense to know better," he added.

"What are you talking about, the ones that ain't got enough sense to know better? And what the hell are you doing back here? Why aren't you out looking for them?"

Slater stopped and looked back toward Buford. "I told you when all this started that it wasn't my fight."

"But I'm paying you to make it your fight," Buford said.

"A hundred dollars, hell, even a thousand dollars ain't enough money to get yourself killed for. They're your problem, not mine. And if you want to find them, my advice is just to hang around here. They seem pretty determined to get to you. More'n likely they're going to show up right here. And when they do, I don't want to be nowhere around.''

"You son of a bitch! You work for me! You can't just walk away like this!'' Buford shouted angrily.

Slater turned his back to Buford, and started toward the bunkhouse. "Oh, no? Watch me walk away,'' he called back over his shoulder.

"You cowardly bastard!'' Buford shouted. He pulled his pistol and shot Slater, hitting him in the back of the head. Slater went down, dead before he hit the ground.

"My God!'' Jessica gasped. She had been watching the entire scene from just inside the front door. "You just shot your own foreman!''

"The sonofabitch was a coward,'' Buford growled. He punched the expended cartridge out of his pistol and replaced it with a new one. "Get back inside and stay out of sight,'' he ordered.

As it developed, Win and Joe had enjoyed a front-row seat to the shooting from their position on a hill about fifty yards from the house. Their inclination was to go up to the house and settle it now, but they had already encountered so many of Buford's men that they didn't know whether there were more back here waiting for them. The brothers' caution was well served when they saw four men running from the bunkhouse, drawn to the scene by the gunfire.

"Son of a bitch!'' one of them shouted, looking at the man on the ground. "This here is Slater! Slater's been kilt!''

"What happened to Slater?'' one of the men asked.

"I killed him,'' Buford said calmly.

"You kilt him? Why?''

"Because the son of a bitch needed killin','' Buford said

as if that were explanation enough. "Now, you men get rifles and take cover. When the Coulters come riding in here they'll be easy targets, and the offer I made to the ones who are out looking for them goes for you too. I'll pay one thousand dollars to see both Coulters dead."

IT WAS NO MORE THAN HALF AN HOUR LATER WHEN WIN and Joe got an unexpected break. Some of the cowboys who had been out on the range searching for the two brothers were now coming back to the ranch. They were tired, hungry, and frustrated over not yet having won any money, and they rode boldly and noisily right up to the ranch. Unfortunately for them, they made no effort to identify themselves.

Those who had remained behind were so nervous that they were jumping at every shadow. They had completely forgotten about the ones who were out on the range, and were totally surprised to see a large body of men ride up on them. It was too dark to see, and they had been made too edgy by the circumstances to exercise the proper caution. One of them put into words what all of them thought.

"Oh, shit! Look at that! The Coulters have rounded up an entire army!"

A rifle shot rang out from one of the ones back at the ranch, and it was returned by the approaching horsemen, who thought they were being fired at by the Coulter brothers. Their return shot was answered by another, and another still, until soon the entire valley rang with the crash and clatter of rifle and pistol fire. Gun flashes lit up the night, and bullets whistled, whined, and thunked into horseflesh, or buried themselves deep into the chests of some of the hapless cowboys.

"Joe!" Win shouted. "Now's our chance! Let's go!"

As the guns banged and crashed around them, the two

brothers sneaked out of their hiding position. They mounted, then rode north for a couple of hundred yards in order to get out of the line of fire. Win had no intention of getting either one of them shot by accident.

Then, during the confusion of the firefight, Win and Joe made plans as to how they would get into the house.

"Look there, maybe we can use that," Joe said, pointing. "That gully winds around all the way up to the barn."

"Yes, but even if we get the barn, we will still have fifty yards of open territory to reach the house," Win said.

"What if I go alone?" Joe suggested. "I'll burn the barn."

"Burn it?"

"Yes. Once it catches fire, it will create a big enough distraction to let you get into the house without being noticed."

Win smiled. "Little Brother, that is a brilliant idea," he said. "All right, do it. But be careful."

Joe nodded, then took a deep breath and started running up the gully, keeping his head low. Win watched him until Joe disappeared in the dark.

Shortly after Joe disappeared, the ranch hands discovered the fact that they had been carrying on a gunfight with themselves. After much calling and shouting, the shooting finally stopped.

"You dumb bastards! You were shooting at us!" someone called.

"Well, you come ridin' in here without a word. What the hell were we to think?"

"Do you think the Coulters would've come ridin' in like that? Goddamn, you've done killed Andy and Deekus. And Tony's lyin' back there somewhere gutshot!"

"Yeah, well, you kilt Frank."

"Too bad we didn't kill all of you, you dumb bastards!"

"Holy shit! Look at the barn! The barn's on fire!" some-one called.

Win looked toward the barn and smiled. Joe had made it, and now flames were climbing up one corner, licking against the dry shake-shingle roof.

"What the hell! How'd that get started?"

Win made his move then. Running low and crouched over, he darted through the darkness, unseen, to the side of the house. He moved through a grape arbor to the back of the house, then slipped inside through the back door.

"Get some buckets! Get some water on that!"

Inside the house, Win was able to use the ambient light of the burning barn to pick his way through the downstairs. When he reached the parlor he got the shock of his life. He saw Jessica, looking through the window toward the burning barn.

"Jessica!" he gasped in surprise. "What the hell! What are you doing here?"

"Win!" Jessica said, turning toward him. Her face registered shame and fear at having been discovered by him.

"She is with me," Buford said from behind Win. When he turned, he saw the big man holding a gun and smiling evilly at him. "Drop your gun, please."

Win held his pistol for a moment longer, then dropped it and looked back at Jessica. "Are you his prisoner?" he asked, though even as he was asking the question he knew that she wasn't.

Buford laughed. "My prisoner?" he said. "Tell him, my dear. Are you my prisoner?"

Jessica stared at the floor.

"I guess she's just a little too embarrassed to tell you that she warms my bed. I mean, being as we aren't married or anything."

"Still following the money, I see, Jessica," Win said.

"Win, you don't understand," Jessica said, her voice racked with guilt.

"You're right, I don't understand," Win said. "Buford I understand, but not you."

"Actually, I'm using Buford as a first name out here," Buford said. "I prefer to be called Lane." He laughed. "However, there really is no need for you to remember that, since you won't be alive long enough to use it."

Buford made a motion toward the door with his pistol. "Now step outside," he ordered. "Step outside and call to your brother. He is the one who set fire to the barn, isn't he? A clever ruse that, burning the barn to give you the chance to sneak into the house. Tell him to give himself up."

"My brother will never give himself up."

"Not even to save your life?"

"Bullshit, Buford. Do you really think he doesn't know you are going to kill me anyway? No. He will do exactly what I would do. He'll stay out there in the dark and watch you kill me. Then he'll kill you. If he can't kill you tonight, he'll kill you tomorrow, or the day after that, or the day after that. But I promise you, he will kill you."

"Get out there," Buford ordered, pushing him from behind.

With Buford shoving him along, Win stepped through the front door and out onto the porch of the house. By now the porch was well lighted by the fire from the burning barn, but none of Buford's riders saw them come out, since they were now involved in a futile effort to put out the burning barn.

"Call to your brother," Buford hissed. "Tell him to show himself."

"If you're going to shoot me, you sonofabitch, do it and

get it over with," Win growled. "I'm not going to call my brother for you."

"Very well, then you shall have your wish. I'll shoot you now."

From behind him, Win heard the double metallic click of Buford's pistol being cocked, and he waited for the bullet to come crashing into the back of his head.

"No!" Jessica suddenly screamed, her scream coming on top of the sound of a gunshot. Win whirled around at the same moment, and saw that Jessica had jumped between Buford and him just as the gun had gone off. Now she was staggering away from Buford, her face racked with pain, her chest covered with blood.

"You stupid whore!" Buford roared. He pointed his gun at her, and was about to shoot her a second time. That gave Win the opening he needed, and he closed the distance between himself and Buford in an instant. He grabbed Buford's arm, forcing the gun up just as he fired a second time. This time the bullet went harmlessly into the roof of the porch.

Buford was so surprised by the sudden move that Win was able to snatch the gun from him. But since he was unable to bring the pistol around into firing position, Win did the next best thing. He brought it crashing down on Buford's head, dropping him to the porch deck like a sack of flour.

"Hey, it's Coulter! There he is, up on the porch!" one of the few remaining cowboys shouted, and they started across the yard from the burning barn. Suddenly, from behind them, another gun roared, and Joe jumped out from behind a wagon.

"Hold it right there, boys!" he shouted. "Drop your guns, all of you."

By now Win had managed to bring the pistol around so

that he too had the drop on the four remaining cowboys. Realizing they were covered, front and back, they had no choice but to do as they were told.

"What do we do now?" one of the men asked.

"Well, you can do one of two things," Win replied.

"What's that?"

"You can die for this sonofabitch or"—he paused for a moment—"you can figure that too many of you have already died for him, and you can get on your horses and ride away."

"I don't know about the rest of you boys," one of the men said. "But this one ain't too hard for me to figure. I'm gettin' the hell out of here."

"Me too," one of the others said.

Moments later, nothing remained of the four cowboys but the sound of receding hoofbeats.

Buford, who had been temporarily knocked out, was now coming to. Groggily, he sat up, rubbing the bump on his head.

"Keep him covered," Win said to Joe as he walked over to examine Jessica. She was breathing her last.

"Win," she said. "I'm sorry. I didn't know it would turn out like this. Can you ever find it in your heart to forgive me?"

"There's nothing to forgive," Win said. "You just saved my life."

Jessica coughed, and bubbles of blood frothed from her lips. "Hold me, Win. Hold . . ." Her head flopped to one side and the gasping breaths and bubbles of blood stopped.

"Damn," Win said. He laid her down on the porch, then stood up and looked down at her. "Damn," he said again.

"What do you want to do with Sergeant Angus Buford here?" Joe asked.

"Shoot the son of a bitch," Win said disgustedly.

Joe cocked his pistol and put it to Buford's head.

"No, wait a minute!" Win suddenly said. He looked at Buford with a sardonic smile. "*Sergeant* Buford, I seem to recall one of your calling cards. I think it might be very appropriate right here."

FIFTEEN MINUTES LATER, WIN AND JOE RODE AWAY FROM the house, a burlap bag full of money hanging from Win's saddle pommel. Behind them, the barn was fully engulfed in fire, and its bright light cast flickering shadows upon the bodies of the half a dozen men and one woman who had been killed there that night.

"No, wait!" Buford was screaming. "Don't go! You can't leave me like this!"

Angus Buford's big frame, back-lighted by the burning barn, was standing on a wagon tongue. Around his neck was a rope, the other end of which was tied to the high branch of a cottonwood tree. Already, flames were licking at the wagon. It was only a matter of time until the tongue, weakened by the fire, would snap in two.

"You bastards! You bastards!" Buford screamed in terror and anger.

Neither Win nor Joe looked back.

AN EPIC NOVEL OF AMERICA IN THE MAKING

CRIPPLE CREEK

●

They came from all across America, many of them recent
immigrants—all of them in pursuit of the same dream. They
came with their mining tools sharpened and their hopes
high. Working hard all day in the dangerous mines, they
were fired by thoughts of a brighter future. They left their
homes and families to find a land of opportunity of their
very own. Many paid a high price for following their
dreams. They found only hardship in the depths of the
mines—and greed and deception in the hearts of others.
But for a lucky few, the golden dream became a
sparkling reality...

Douglas Hirt
__0-425-15850-0/$5.99